A
Flock
of
Shadows

Parthian
The Old Surgery
Napier Street
Cardigan
SA43 1ED
www.parthianbooks.com

First published by Parthian in 2014
© Contributors
All Rights Reserved
'Mia' first published by the Rattle Tales Group in *Rattle Tales*,
2014.

ISBN 978-1-909844-88-9

The publisher acknowledges the financial support of
the Welsh Books Council.

Editing and cover design by Claire Houguez and Rebecca Parfitt

Typesetting by Claire Houguez
Printed and bound by Lightningsource.com

A Flock of Shadows

13 Tales of the Contemporary Gothic

Edited by
Claire Houguez & Rebecca Parfitt

PARTHIAN

Contents

Foreword

Sick of sighing at the namby-pampy vampires and hipster witches in mainstream fiction? Of the supernatural stoically resisting its own evil? Parthian and *The Ghastling* decided to take matters into our own hands with a call to arms for some proper gothic fiction.

In poured ghost stories, the macabre and the spine-tinglingly strange, with clipped contemporary prose and classic, expansive tones. *A Flock of Shadows* gathers and celebrates current gothic voices – after all, there's safety in numbers.

Let us now appear – out of nowhere, cloaked, by your elbow – and, like a mysterious hawker, spread our exotic wares before disappearing into the night again…

No gothic anthology is complete without a brooding house, but you'll find no mist-veiled moorlands here. In Kate North's 'Fifteen Arthur Crescent', this is an ordinary street; the events of this story could happen to any one of us. North unfolds a tale that disquiets and unnerves the reader as they settle into an armchair in the cosiness of their living room… and brings a whole new meaning to 'house proud'.

Who cares that a house isn't a conventional lover? Allow the entrapped inhabitant of Carly Holmes' 'Piece by Piece' to show you proudly around a rather captivating home. A strange, obsessive relationship emerges during the tour of gleaming colours and caressed cornices.

Rhys Owain Willams' 'The Office Block' is a drift through somnambulant days and quiet night hours plagued by insomnia and the steady oppressive torment of the watchful building opposite. In *A Flock of Shadows*, buildings come to oppressive life, demand more than lovers, pursue their own malevolent intents.

Fans of classic ghost stories must hasten to Jo Mazelis' 'Storm Dogs', which brings a word of warning to the traveller: beware of the seemingly kindly intentions of strangers, as what at first appears charitable may come with a heavy price. In this strange and hypnotic tale, set in 1950s France against the backdrop of a magnificent chateaux, a charm befalls the travellers and as events unfold so does a terrible accident… or is it?

There's also murder and madness aplenty in this collection. Mark Blayney's 'The Wednesday Ghost' dips us in the dreamlike space of an artist attempting to come to terms with having murdered one of his models. But is all really as it seems in this shifting space of subjective reality and artifice?

Paula Readman's audacious 'The Gardener' drops us into the chillingly reasonable narrative of a single-minded botanist that, guided by her knowledge of the rare and poisonous, will stop at nothing to protect her beloved borders. But then the rumors begin…

In Alan Bilton's unsettling, darkly comic tale 'The Alphabet's Shadow', a couple struggle to communicate through the separate liminal spaces of grief, a beloved lost pet may have returned in a twilit park, and mysterious maps appear in strange places. But where are they leading?

Morgan Downie's 'Enter the Petal Throne' collects the fragmented experience of the absinthe drinker. A story, swimming with vivid imagery, evoking opulence akin to the smoke-filled jazz era, that assures: 'To know what we want

[...] is merely a matter of admitting to oneself.' But what if you don't know? An 'indecisive' goes in search of the future, seeking advice inside a peculiar place – a shop that sells dreams and fortunes. The seeker surrenders his own reality and enters a place that he later finds he is unable to leave.

And we've a host of otherworldly creatures for you. Can a woman really 'intoxicate' with her charms? In Amanda Mason's 'Mia', yes, and the victim, who only tries to save the seemingly vulnerable young innocent, ends up seeking darkness himself.

Shirley Golden's 'Singing a New Song' is gothic horror of a different kind: it confronts the monstrosity of war. In the misery of the trenches, soldiers fight for survival against bullets, wire, rats and fleas. But one soldier is less concerned with mortality. The smell of blood excites his senses. This story unfolds between the blurred lines of good and evil, the monstrous reality and the monstrous imagined. In war, all horrors are believable, *all* horrors are real... 'The shadow of absolute evil is no longer the fear. Good or bad depends upon which side of the parapet your head appears'.

Howard Ingham's tale 'Why the Others Were Taken' blends the everyday horrors of a dysfunctional family with the truly incomprehensible, unleashed by the arrival of an unexpected and grisly visitor. This story blends the best of the classic and contemporary gothic fiction forms, and it's slow build of emotion is truly disquieting.

Is the figure of the beautiful, hair-combing mermaid really an accurate representation? The beauty of the creature of Laura Wilkinson's story 'Towards the Sea' certainly seems firmly lodged in the eye of the beholders, who regal the local barmaid with the tall tales of their lustful encounters. But the barmaid has her own intimate knowledge.

And last but not least, as they say, come the exotic monstrosities of Bethany W. Pope's 'The Silver Wire', in which a bored nanny torments her charge with stories – and not the good ones. Stories of crones and the Aswang, whose eyes are red from not sleeping because at night they turn into black dogs and eat children and corpses. And of the Manananggal, the baby-stealing creature that just may come for the child's own pregnant mother.

We hope to have piqued your curiosity – a trait that never lead anyone into real trouble… The oldest and strongest emotion of mankind is fear and what we each fear says so much about us. Which story will leave you haunted?

Why the Others Were Taken

 ou have to understand, says my father, that your grandmother was not a bad woman. She saw a lot of tragedy in her life.

My father is standing in his sitting room holding an open Tupperware box, in which he has deposited broken bits of cheesy Quaver, limp white cucumber and lettuce sandwiches, abandoned party-size sausage rolls harvested from the coffee table and the settee. Beyond practical arrangements for the funeral, this is the first opinion that Dad has expressed regarding his mother-in-law since I got back here.

My father's house — I grew up here — I stopped thinking about it as 'home' a long time ago — has been more or less silent for half an hour. Now that the wake is over, we are making the house presentable again.

Dad doesn't have a dishwasher. My hands are red and a bit wrinkly. I have splashed water on my dress. I came back in to ask him where the salad bowls go. The cupboards are all arranged differently now. I haven't lived here for a long time.

I put the glass bowl down on the coffee table. I can't think of an appropriate response. He's been crying. I have never seen him cry and it takes a moment to recognise it — the red eyes, the shininess on the cheeks.

— *Dad*, I say.

I know he isn't crying for Nan.

Bang. The sound of a fist on the front door echoes through the house. Dad stiffens. It comes again, bang, and he looks away from me, face contorted. A third time: bang. A fourth: bang. Four more: bang, bang, bang, bang.

— *I'll get that*, I say.

Four more again: bang, bang, bang, bang.

— *No*, he says. *I think I'd rather you didn't.*

*

The last time I had spoken properly to my Nan was on the day of my mother's funeral. This was six months ago. I had been up to talk to her a few times already, and I had told her how sorry I was that her daughter — not my mother, her daughter — had died so suddenly. She had been dismissive and cold. I had brought her several cups of tea; she had not thanked me. I had come to offer to drive her to Mum's funeral, to push the wheelchair; she had refused.

I had left her sitting up in bed in her room at the top of my parents' stairs, staring at the gaps in the yellow wallpaper on the wall opposite, hand clasped in her lap like a little heap of kindling. I had stood at the lectern in the Chapel of Rest and had read the fourteenth chapter of John's Gospel to the assembled mourners: *In my house are many rooms. If it were not so, I would have told you. I go now to prepare a place for you.* I imagined Nan, the whole time, in the bed, scowling into space.

After the burial, when I returned, she was still in that position. I said, *Hello, Nan*, and she didn't move, so I repeated myself, and she said, without looking at me,

— *I 'eard you the first time, maid.*

— *How are you, Nan?*

– *How d'ye bleddy think I am, ye bleddy fool?*

I bit my lip. I rested my hand on the back of my neck, looked down at a stain on the carpet.

– *Nan*, I said, *Uncle Derek is here. He wanted to come and see you.*

She stared at the wall.

– *Derek, Nan.*

She sucked on her lips for a moment.

– *'E can pess right off.*

– *Nan –*

– *No, 'e had his chance. 'E coulda come back any time. Too late for 'im now. Too late. 'E can't come back begging now. 'E en't tekken anymore from me, you 'ear me? He can pess right off. Tell him to pess off, maid.*

I wanted to hit her. I wanted to say, get yourself a sense of proportion, you evil old baggage. I wanted to say, it should be you who died. I said,

– *All right.*

And I went downstairs, and I left Dad to deal with her, and three days later I went home without once opening the door at the top of the stairs or saying goodbye.

And the day after I went home, Nan had the first of a dozen or more minor strokes, and her mind and the last of her control over her body went, in the space of a week. Dad, denied the time to mourn Mum, spent the next six months nursing her.

I wondered sometimes if Nan was punishing him for loving her daughter.

*

When the echo of the knocks has subsided, Dad sits down on the table, holding the plastic box on his lap, and presses the thumb and first finger of one hand into his eyes. He sighs.

Then he snaps to, puts the box on the table, stands off, walks out of the room.

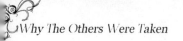

 — *I'm making tea*, he says. He heads to the kitchen.
I follow.
 — *Dad*, I say, *What just happened?*
 — *It's probably just kids.*
 — *So what, it's happened before?*
 — *Every so often, yes.*
 — *And you never answered it?*
 — *No.*
 — *Oh, good grief. How long has this been going on, Dad?*
 — *Since your mother went. Two or three times a week.*
 — *Have you called the police or anything?*
 — *No. They just bang on the door. Nothing ever happens. No one does anything.*

He's shaking. Some of the tea spills on the worktop.
 — *Oh, Dad.*

I leave it for a moment. Then, I try to sit him down with his tea while I finish the tidying. He isn't having any of it.

*

Nan had been in the bed in Mum and Dad's spare room for about a year — there was no question of being able to afford a place in a home — when Mum re-established contact with Uncle Derek. She never told me how, just that it was an accident, a coincidence. In the space of a minute, an older brother Mum had not seen for fifty years stumbled, politely apologising, back into her life.

Mum had gone, still in tears, to tell her mother that she had just seen Derek, and Nan had said, *So what?* And Mum had said, *But it's Derek*, and Nan had said that what is buried and dead must remain buried and dead.

Nan lived by that phrase, or claimed to.

*

— *It was good of Derek to come*, I say. *After... everything.*

— *He couldn't do any less.* Dad puts his mug down. He grew up using tea leaves and even though he's used teabags for years, he always leaves a bit at the bottom.

— *He'd have been justified in not coming.*

— *It was his duty. It doesn't matter what she did. She was his mother.*

— *I thought she wasn't to blame for what happened.*

— *Oh, your Nan had her part.*

I am surprised for a moment at the depth of feeling in my father's statement, that he, a man so cautious, so softly spoken, so unwilling to speak ill of the dead, especially the dead, might be able today of all days to say something about that vile old woman that is true.

— *So what actually happened, Dad?*

He leans over and picks up the mug, looks into it, puts it down, looks at me. His fingers twitch like he is about to light a cigarette, but he gave up years ago, so he looks uncomfortable and licks his lips and says,

— *Well.*

And then the banging on the door starts again.

*

At some time during the Second World War, when my mother was barely even walking, all of her four older brothers and sisters were taken away by the Social, and put into an orphanage.

Mum was an evacuee. During the Blitz, she was sent to the country, and when the bombing raids were over, she came back home to a home she was too young to have remembered the first time, and to the first of three younger siblings. Before her evacuation, she was the youngest of five; now she was the eldest of four. Her mother was not even thirty when the youngest was born.

When they had come of age, the four elder children, now grown, came back. They argued with their parents and bullied my mother, and then, as soon as each found some place to go, one by one they went away and did not come back, and only they and my grandparents knew why this had happened. But they had gone away, and Nan and Grandad would not ever speak of the others again, or even admit that they had existed.

*

Bang. Bang. Bang. Bang.

Dad puts out a hand, but I am on my feet and sprinting for the door and I am furious, ready to thump someone. I snatch the key off the hook and fumble with the lock and ball my fists and draw in breath ready to scream abuse at my father's tormentor.

The smell hits me in the face, stops me in my tracks. I recoil, back of my hand to my mouth, eyes immediately watering.

The figure on the doorstep judders; clods of earth fall on to the doorstep. I do not recognise her. Dad is behind me; I did not notice him there. He pushes next to me and says, in a small, sad voice,

— *Moira?*

For a moment, I wonder who Moira is, if my father knew another Moira. Dad says the name again. And I choke and hold my gorge down as it comes to me.

— *Mum*, I say.

Dad is leaning on me. He is swaying. I put my arm around him, prop him up.

And then Mum, six months dead and standing on my doorstep, with the earth of the grave on the tattered dress and her fingertips ripped and bloodied, with the little mole on the side of her nose and the two rings on the third finger of her left hand... Mum begins to scream.

I am unable to move beyond supporting the near-dead weight of my father, and it is his weight that brings me back to myself, and my mum stops screaming. She judders again. More earth thuds to the ground, explodes on the doorstep.

The head turns a fraction, and eyes the colour of month-old milk stare at me. She opens her mouth, as if to speak. Nothing comes out apart from a wet rattle.

Dad straightens up, draws in breath. He pushes me gently to one side and takes Mum's hand gently in his, leads her past me. She stumbles, rights herself, drags one foot. Dad leads her inside into the lounge. I look up and down the street and shut the door.

— *She's cold*, says Dad. *She's really cold.*

He sends me upstairs to get a blanket. I stare at him for a minute, but I cannot think of anything else to do, so I go, and soon Mum is sat on the sofa with a blanket around her and we are at a loss as to what to do next.

We sit with Mum until dawn, and she says nothing, and stares into space, and sometimes she rattles. The lights are all on, but the corners of the room seem very dark.

*

At about nine in the morning, I make some tea. I am not thinking. I pour four cups, put three of them onto a tray, take them into the lounge, turn to go back into the kitchen.

— *I was just —* I stop myself.

— *What?* says Dad.

— *I made another cup. For — I was going to take it to —* I shake my head.

Dad is staring at me.

Making sure not to look at the door at the top of the stairs, I return to the kitchen, pour it down the sink.

Mum doesn't drink hers. When it has cooled down a little, Dad tries to get her to drink some by holding the cup to her mouth, but it trickles out the sides.

– *Right*, says Dad. *This can't go on. She's smells awful. She's filthy.*

It's the damp metallic sort of smell that earth has, the smell that grits up the back of your throat, a taste that reminds you of things you would never willingly eat, like mould and earthworms, all mixed in with something else, something unfamiliar and queasy. She smells like she's crawled out of the ground.

What can we do? We lead her upstairs and we give her a bath. I leave Dad to undress her – I can't, she's my Mum – but it's up to me to pick her up like a baby and lift her into the water. She is very light. Fragile and awkward, like an armful of swept-up leaves. I keep expecting her to fall apart in my hands. When she hits the water, she begins to scream again. Dad steadies himself on the door frame, turns, stumbles, falls to his knees on the landing, vomits on the carpet.

– *Dad?* I don't know if I should leave Mum or go to him. I try to call out over the screaming. *Dad, are you OK?*

He is already on his feet and heading for the stairs. Mum stops screaming.

– *I'm going to get some disinfectant and a bucket*, he says.

I turn to Mum and start to try to clean her up. Her teeth are yellow. Her skin is greyish and pockmarked with deep, bloodless, ragged holes. And out of those sour-milk eyes leak viscous white tears.

I can see a snail floating in the bath.

I reach in and take Mum's hand, lift it, stroke it gently.

– *It's all right, Mum. It's OK. It's all going to be fine.*

She turns and looks at me with those terrible opaque eyes, mouth hanging open. She rattles again.

– *Mum?*

And she rattles again. Dad comes back in. Mum looks up at him. Her hands splash feebly in the bath as she does so.

– *Dad, I think she knows.*

– *Oh, God*, he says. *Oh, God. Moira?*

She begins to scream again.

*

My mother, now cleaned up and dressed in clothes my Dad could never bring himself to give to a charity shop or throw away like he said he had, is lying on the couch. Dad is perched on the end, stroking her forehead the way he used to when she had a migraine. Occasionally, she rattles and twitches.

When the phone rings, she starts again to scream, until Dad takes her hand and whispers soothingly to her. I head to the kitchen to get it.

It's Derek.

– *Is your Dad there, Jan?*

– *Um, he's sort of busy. Can I take a message?*

– *No, I can tell you. It's probably better I tell you. You're blood.*

– *What's wrong?*

– *Well, nothing. Everything. Listen. I don't know you so well, but you're Moira's. And that matters. I wanted to say goodbye. That's all.*

I say nothing. He can hear me breathing.

– *I tried. To put things right with Mother – your grandmother, I mean –* He tails off.

– *I understand*, I say.

– *Yes, I think you do. I had to do right by her. At the funeral. But.*

I know where this is going.

– *I am sorry I couldn't say earlier, Jan. To be honest, I have only just decided. I owe it to you and Eric to tell you.*

For a second, I want to say to him, *Let me put Mum on*, but I know that's insane, and it would damage him, damage his own grief, not only for his sister but for his life.

— *I never told your mother why, Jan.*

Decades of hurt, several generations' worth. And it all boils down to that one little *why.*

— *I wrote a letter, he says. I never gave it to her. I want you to have it. You won't have to read it if you don't want to. But —*

— *I know,* I say.

— *I think it's better if we cut off contact now. I don't have anything against you. I just think I need to draw a line under that part of my life.*

— *I understand,* I say. *It was a privilege to meet you, Uncle Derek.*

— *I am not sure that you're right. Still, I've sent it now. I don't know. Maybe it should have been buried.*

The hairs on the back of my neck stand up. I suddenly become aware that I am not alone in the kitchen. I am very cold. I do not turn around. I fix my gaze to the little orange display on the phone cradle.

— *I know,* I say.

I imagine a hand touching my shoulder.

— *Good luck, Jan. Send my regards to your father.*

I will not turn around.

— *Goodbye, Uncle Derek. And thank you.*

He hangs up. I put the receiver back on the cradle and I stand there silently, transfixed, my hand still on the receiver —

I whirl around. It's eleven in the morning, but the kitchen is dark. The shadows spread, even as I watch, from the corners of the room, leak around the edges.

I swallow.

I walk slowly to the sink, and I fill the kettle and I put it on, and I make a pot of tea. By the time I leave the kitchen with two mugs of tea, I can feel the shadows brushing against my skin, like the frail, paper-dry fingers of someone very old.

I stop at the bottom of the stairs, look up. The door to Nan's room is so covered in shadows it cannot be seen at all.

*

I don't know how long we've been here now, Dad and me, sitting here next to Mum, me on the floor, Dad still perched on the couch. It feels like days. We haven't slept or washed. Neither of us has eaten anything substantial apart from a few leftovers. We have up to now subsisted on tea and biscuits, but the milk is running out, and we finished the last of the biscuits, even the Rich Teas, some time ago. It's so dark in here. All the lights are on.

Neither of us has any idea what time it is. We have an unspoken, irrational agreement not to open the curtains, and it is unclear to me whether that is to keep people outside from seeing in or to keep us seeing what might be outside. We might have sat through a second night. Maybe even a third. We don't know.

When the letterbox goes, we're both surprised. Neither of us thought it was morning.

    — *One of us should get that*, says Dad.

    — *Yeah*, I say.

    — *Jan*, says Dad, *I don't think I can.*

    — *It's OK, Dad.*

Mum rattles.

I stand up and take a breath. I step into the shadows. They paw at me weakly, breathe on me with a smell like old cabbage and cigarettes and poverty. They are only shadows.

The hall stretches in front of me for miles. I cannot see the front door. Just Dad's tatty, faded carpet. Just Dad's magnolia walls, fading into the distance, into the dark.

    — *I don't care, Nan*, I say out loud. *I don't care.*

And now I am sitting on the doormat with my back against the front door with a handful of post: a condolence card from someone I have never heard of; a bank statement; a charity mass-mailer, the sort where they include the cheap ballpoint pen so you have no excuse but to fill in the form; and a letter addressed to Mum. I drop the rest of the post on the floor and look at it in both hands.

The shadows snake out of the air and try to snatch it from me, but they are just shadows. I pick it up, unopened, and return to the lounge through the frustrated dark.

When I reach Dad and Mum, I open the letter and say, *This is for you, Mum*, and I begin to read it to her, and before I have finished she is screaming again. Dad has his hands clamped over his ears.

It is long. It explains everything. The room gets darker as I read it. I do not stop. When I finish, Mum's screams subside to a constant rattling, which rises and subsides in waves, which has the rhythm of something sobbing.

The darkness stretches forward, threatens to engulf us all completely.

I walk into it, and I run up the stairs three steps at a time, and I stand outside Nan's door and I call in:

— *We know, Nan! We know what happened. We know why. We know why, Nan, and I don't care. Stop punishing us for this. It happened thirty years before I was born, Nan. Derek's moved on. It's nothing to do with Dad anymore. No one else is alive who cares, Nan. Stop punishing us. And stop punishing Mum, Nan. No one cares. Do you hear me? No one cares!*

I am crying out at the top of my voice, and I stop only when inside the room I hear crashes and bangs, the sounds of splintering wood and smashing glass. The door bangs as something hits it hard from the other side, and then it stops and there is silence, and the house is in daylight again.

But the screaming continues downstairs, and I realise that this time it's Dad.

When I get to the lounge door the smell, worse than ever, assaults me, and across the sofa is something made of mud and slime and bones and disintegrating, worm-ridden meat, and Dad stops screaming and straightens up and he has parts of my mother's decaying flesh all down his front, over his hands and up his arms, and he has tears streaming down his face, and he is yelling at me in a broken, shrill voice: *What did you do?*

What did you do?

Piece By Piece

hen you walk into this room pause for a moment, please, and look around you. Don't simply scan for walls that can be knocked through, don't just take mental measurement of the march from skirting board to skirting board and wonder how your greedy four-seater sofa will ever fit. Look down first, past the scuff of your leather shoes, and see how rich, how varied, the brown of the floorboards is. The grain carries every shade between mocha and bistre depending on the time of day. When the afternoon sun warms the wood, believe me, you'll feel an urge to take off your clothes and lay stretched across it, legs splayed as wide as they can get. You'll sink into it, deep down to the memory of its living roots, and you'll dream of burrowing mice and earthworms. In the early morning chill you'll need slippers, or socks at the very least, before you'll dare to tread its sharp, forest length, and even then you'll think of wolves and thorns and fear for fragile toes.

It didn't get this gleam by chance, you know. It was me. It was love. And hours of polishing, sliding around on my knees, queasy from the fumes. I massaged and I stroked and I drew its colours back to the surface whenever they started to flatten and fade. I talked to it the whole time. My hands would be so cramped after I'd finished, I wouldn't be able to straighten my fingers for the rest of the day, but it was worth it. The floorboards sighed their delight and rubbed themselves against the pat of my palms, nudging my flesh until there was nothing else to do but take my clothes back off and use my body to smooth in the top coat of polish.

Look up now and see the painted walls lighten as they drop to knee height. I did that myself, by mixing firebrick into vermilion in increasing amounts. And admire the stencil work up there by the mouldings, so delicate it's almost shadow play. Please don't think about wallpapering over it the moment you move in, you'll never see this shade of red again. I cut my hand when I was getting the lids off the pots and I let my blood drip into the paint. It bled a lot and I stirred it in well. I think it added something special to the mix.

You're interested in the stairs, I can tell. Look at you, you can barely keep your hands to yourself. Go on, swing your leg over the banister and slide down to the newel post, there's no one else around. I used to do that every morning, at the beginning. The sturdiness of the rail between my thighs always made me gasp and shiver. Sometimes, when I should have been on my way to work, I'd run up and slide back down, again and again. I was so playful back then. By the time I was finally settled behind my desk, damp from all the laughing, my hair one long tangle, it would be time for lunch. They let me go in the end but I would have left anyway. There just weren't enough hours in the day, enough days in the week, and I resented every moment spent outside my own front door. I think of them sometimes, my work colleagues, rutting mindlessly in their filthy homes, rolling across carpets stricken with mould, walls collapsing around their ears, and I pity them. Who cares that a house isn't a conventional lover?

You'll see from the flagstones in the kitchen, the cornices in the bedrooms, that this house has been stroked and fondled as much as any human body could ever be. They're almost as perfect as the day they were first fitted, and they're original pieces. But the honeymoon period ended, as it does, and by the time I reached the top floor the easy loving was gone. It wasn't enough anymore to just polish and paint. Gone were the long and sleepless nights when we'd lie together and I'd whisper my dreams into its corners. Gone the naked jiving through from lounge to porch. When I arranged to meet a friend at the pub down the road, just a quick drink, the new pipes I'd installed buckled and flooded the cellar. Boxes of my old diaries ruined. If I hurried to the corner shop to get more milk I'd return to a cold so spiteful my breath gusted from my mouth in dense sharp spikes and the radiators shivered.

I knew I was becoming *less* when I had to stand on a chair to reach the top of the doorframes to dust them. I could slip my arms through the supporting pillars of the banister, right up to the elbow. And then my fingernails began to soften and fall like bruised poppy petals. My hair unscrewed itself from my scalp and flung itself across carpets, across floorboards, across windowsills. By the time I'd finished sweeping and sponging, I had to start over again.

I'd lie awake at night and hear the grunts, the sighs, as the house shifted around me. It groaned as it reached to pull me close and at the same time sharpened its edges to give any offered embrace the sting of rejection. Even the light switches shocked me when I touched them. We were lovers at war and it was too big a foe, too jealous a beloved, to take my softness and leave me uncrushed. My passion stripped the flesh from my skeleton and then started on the very core of me, sucking until I was nothing but gristle and nerves.

My brittling bones, so close to the surface now, elbows and heels piercing skin, more mortar than marrow, brought me down beside the fireplace, here. The house's gaping mouth. Its empty heart. And here I lay, and let it take me, piece by piece.

It was always going to end like this, for me. I loved too much. I didn't know where to draw the line. But for you it could be different. The house just needs a firmer touch, a woman with a bit more backbone. Don't take any of its shit, and don't let it see how much you need it.

And if you do move in, please don't plasterboard over the hearth, and don't touch the mantelpiece. That's where I am now, what's left of me. I huddle into the cracks, crumbled as thin, as dry, as cement dust. But I still remember the feel of the banister between my thighs, the wild joy of laughing for hours, and I don't regret any of it.

The Wednesday Ghost

 suppose I shouldn't have killed her, but when do we ever do what we're supposed to do? I went to the park, as often happens when the images become too intense and saw, just for a moment, a red squirrel. It was a flash, a spiral of burnt orange looping itself around a tree branch, which bounced as the squirrel ran along it before vanishing. I hoped it would reappear, but there was just the familiar trickling stream and an occasional brown leaf floating to earth in its own time. Not a care in the world. Bastard leaf.

There's something cleansing about the vein of blue water running the length of the park, absolving my sins, healing the guilt. Six months and two days now and each morning, the fear of the hammering on the door fades a little.

Spat on by rain I found my gloves and diverted to the ornate gateway that leads to the history museum. This is my favourite arch. Can you have a favourite arch? It looks like stone but after walking through and turning back you see that it's actually plain red brick, plastered on the front to look like granite. Now why has it only been decorated on one side? Is it a sign to be wary of the history within, to turn it over and look at it from both sides, before you believe it? Allusion. Illusion.

Graffiti on the brick side. Bricks are fair target. Stone is respected.

Calm, deadening hush inside the museum. Floor polish smell. I glided through corridors. Glid? Sounds wrong, doesn't it, glided. The occasional distant squeak, as an attendant's high heels glissaded – that's better – across the dark wood floor. A cough from someone absent.

A Max Ernst exhibition on the first floor and as the images became increasingly surreal, I felt myself detach from the high-ceilinged rooms and travel past the lead-latticed windows. The engravings were from *Une semaine de bonté*; I needed the leaflet to discover that 'bonté' means 'kindness'. Each day had its own room. Sunday was bright orange, Tuesday blue, Wednesday yellow. I've always seen Wednesday as a green word. To my surprise, not everyone thinks the same.

One of the captions began with the word 'SO…' in large, Art Nouveau letters, and for a moment I saw this as *50*. A strange age, fifty, and only another few months to go. A decade since I was a young man; a decade until I'll be an old one. And the daily shock of discovering solitude. Sometimes I can squint at this and believe it's healthier, not having to put a shirt on if I don't want to, not having to worry about eating. But if a relationship is a series of compromises, the voluntary adoption of conventions, well. What a price you pay to sidestep convention.

You shouldn't have killed her then, should you, I thought as I reached the third room and saw a man with the head of a bird being devoured by a harpy with angel's wings and chicken's feet. The cough, that I had heard echoing earlier. A woman in her 20s stood at the far end of the room, looking at an engraving of a flamingo with a lion's head, horror-struck as it contemplated a flooded temple. She wore a pale green t-shirt and jeans (the woman, not the lion-flamingo) and had a slender figure, shaped rather like a 7 as she leant forward to study the picture.

I kept out of sight. You can't talk to strangers, Stefan, not now you're a murderer. She didn't notice me anyway, but as my heels squeaked on the way past she looked up and caught my eye. I couldn't help smiling and she held the smile. I paused, suddenly consumed with interest at a locomotive with severed heads emerging from its funnels instead of steam. She smiled a second time; a warm, friendly, nodding smile, almost of recognition.

Have we met before? Surely not. I would remember. I half-opened my mouth and she nodded again, then turned back to her flamingo-lion.

There's only so long you can stare at an engraving of severed-head steam. I squeaked on to the next room. Of course, almost immediately lines now came into my head. 'This place is a bit of a maze, isn't it?' 'What did you think of the room with the giant caterpillars, they're pretty amazing, aren't they?'

The prints in front of me – Thursday I was onto now – swirled and melted into each other. I back-peddled, went into the previous room – but it was too late, she was gone. A serpent with a headdress like a peacock, breasts curiously apple-like, stared at me. A gargoyle clawed a polite husband. There wasn't enough space between the print and the wall; it was screwed in too tightly, impaling it against the plaster. You have to allow a picture to breathe, to let it rise and fall against its home, or it cannot rest. The gargoyle looked like it might fly out at any moment.

She wasn't in the second or first room either – the woman, not the gargoyle. Where had she gone? I retraced my steps to Thursday. Through the exit to the left to the vivid red of Friday. She wasn't there, nor did she hang around for the weekend.

At the far end the revolving door slowly moved round of its own empty volition, the glass panels glittering and flashing as each one in turn caught the light and reflected back upon me.

The museum seemed, and certainly sounded, empty. Why hadn't I spoken to her when I had the chance? And now you'll never see her again. A moment of eternal, existential angst. Ah well. It's your own fault, for being a murderer. Perhaps if I hadn't brutally killed someone in a moment of sudden, scarlet insanity, you'd have been able to speak to her; able to be casual. Like normal people. You just needed to gird your lions – your *loins* – too late now.

I looked at a skeleton welcoming an eagle into its home with exaggerated formality. Next to him, a bowler-hatted fox in a railway carriage looked surprised to have just pulled up next to the Sphinx. Time to go.

The walk home, the nostalgia for earlier decades, stripping themselves like bark from each tree I passed. The beautiful women I knew and courted in my 20s, the velvet-trousered artist, the potential in front of me, and a sexual life opening up like a glittering bowl of fruit. Get a grip, Stef. That phrase, 'empty volition', revolved in my head. It doesn't mean anything, and yet it makes perfect sense.

Perhaps I should go back to exhibition openings again – is it more suspicious to disappear, than to carry on as normal? Does it make the knock at the door more likely, or less? On the way through the gates and onto the Reeperbahn, I seriously contemplated it. But on balance – a firework shot across the road in front of me, skimmed by a high teenager – it would only lead to trouble. People would ask, why did you stop painting – it wouldn't take long to crack.

The firework exploded with a clang on a steel bin. A police truck ambled past, seeing nothing. I glanced back to the park and saw the squirrel again, a streak of red through trees like paint bleeding in from someone else's picture. A red squirrel in the heart of the city; who would believe it?

On the way up to the flat I paused to pick up one of the stale *brünchens* the baker gives me if I come in after 6, and ate it on the second floor, pausing to watch a mist descend across the wasteland. Half an hour later I realised I was cold and looked for my key.

He thought he saw the woman several times. Twice on the street, she was standing in the mid-distance, or on the other side of the road. He saw her in the corner of his eye, almost illuminated, but when he turned to look, there was nothing but passers-by and street hoardings. Everyone seemed to have purpose: collars turned up, newspapers rolled, steam streaming from nostrils like ponies hurrying.

He saw her once more by the entrance to the S-bahn before deciding with some irritation to rid her from his imagination. He was disoriented, as if unsure where he was on the familiar street, even though he'd lived on various roads leading away from it for much of his life. He was as far as the police station before noticing he'd gone a block too far, and retraced his steps.

He thought about her again on Monday when, trying to reinvigorate interest in work, he unlocked the studio and pulled the dustsheet from his current restoration. When Stefan claimed to have left painting behind, perhaps he was being a little melodramatic with you. He does that; it's like his coat with the upturned collar, it's like reminiscing about velvet trousers. It's true that he isn't currently painting, but he hasn't even put his painting equipment away; it still litters his studio, which is still called a studio, and he now restores paintings for a living. Quite a good living, it has to be said.

Today he's working on a vast, long Venice landscape, a Canaletto wannabe, and the most interesting thing about it is its frame. Ornate, detailed and humorous, Stefan often finds his attention straying to its curlicues when he is supposed to be working on a flat gondola or a bendy barber's pole. He feels, and this is his artist's posturing again, that he's worthy of better.

But his clients recognise his skills, and because of his minor local fame, he's well-known and gets the work.

The tiny figures are the only parts of *Reflection by the Doge's Palace* that interest him; their faces pinkly vague and sketched with two or three brushstrokes, the amorphous features giving space for interpretation, for curiosity. A gondolier stares indulgently, or perhaps patronisingly, or maybe lecherously, at his passengers. A tourist looks with interest at the buildings, or in confusion at where he is, or disapprovingly at the excessive display of wealth. Women on the quay, hands on hips; bored, or curious, or disgusted by the sewers. Or are they flirting with the gilded men opposite?

Whatever they're doing, they've all been coated in a thick sticky varnish, sometime in the late nineteenth century and removing this is the bulk of Stefan's task. Everyone was at it at the time, protecting the paintings for future generations, they thought; but the varnish evolves from transparent to sepia over the decades. The result is countless paintings that now squint on the world through a brown, toffee-wrapping filter. And despite knowing how much difference the restoration process can make, Stefan is still frequently surprised by what emerges from his work. Indiscriminate greys on dresses become bright viridian greens. Dark swarthy gypsies transform into fresh porcelain beauties. Occasionally, brand new figures appear from the murk – a black dog, or a shadowy companion.

There are different techniques for certain colours, because the pigments respond to the cleaning chemicals in different ways; so Stefan addresses a particular block of colour at a time. One process to lift the varnish, another to clean the colour, and only then does he take the opportunity to repair cracks or damage where appropriate. He saves these 'fun bits'. It breaks the day up, keeps him going, and the job briefly becomes more art than science. How much is too much? When does conservation become re-making, when is an invisible line crossed where he's imposing his own creativity on the artist's?

Sometimes the owners of the paintings (it's usually museums, but there are a surprising number of private owners hidden away behind ordinary facades) ask him to do everything he can to improve them; particularly if the artist isn't well-known, or the painting badly damaged. The public-owned galleries, on the other hand, only want the barest minimum done. Remove the varnish; detach dirt; err on the side of caution.

The work is slow, tedious. Punishment for being an unpunished murderer. And by embracing the boredom rather than resisting it, he can reach a level of serenity and calm that might be described as happiness; were it not for the nagging sense that he's not doing what he should be doing in life. You were a highly regarded painter, he tells himself; you could have become a great one. Well tough; being a murderer has changed things. And restoration is a more nurturing career for someone still recovering from trauma. This serenity can last hours, before the searing red images flash on his skull again and the head-in-hands screaming leads his neighbours, above below and sideways, to conclude a maniac lives next door, and/or someone with a very colourful sex life.

A coded knock on the door – always knock with a pattern, Stefan has told his friends, although he hasn't told them why (they just think he's eccentric) – and he is glad of the excuse to pull the dustsheet over the painting and send the harbour into night-time.

'How's it going?' Jan asked.

Stefan shrugged. 'Like the boring bits on a jigsaw. Too much sky. Water. Too much caramel wedding cake.'

Jan raised his eyebrows at the brown, painty dustsheet. 'Eh?'

'I mean Doge's Palace.'

'Ah.'

'How are you?'

'I'm fine.' Jan munched on a *brünchen*. 'Someone's just given me this, can you believe it?'

'What's it like?'

'Bit stale. Still, it's free.' He ate it valiantly. They went to a bar on the Silbersack.

In the morning he accepted two offers of work and spent a further five or six hours beside the Venice harbour. Around lunchtime an unexpected burst of sun broke through the rain and lit the eagles on pillars, their gold suddenly restored to brightness. Stefan adjusted the blinds and returned to a particularly wonky boat, which when he looked at it kept a figure on the quayside just in the corner of his eye.

Each time he focused on the gondola, the figure resolved itself into the woman from the museum. She smiled quizzically, beckoning him forward. Glancing towards her, however, she assumed her former faceless, plastic gawp. Back to the gondola and there she was again, half-smiling, almost insolent. Look at me, she seemed to say. Look at me.

Just forget about her, he told himself. But she remained, indisputably her, as long as she was on the edge of his vision, resuming her anonymity whenever he looked towards her. Eventually he gave up and went out.

She was in the street too. I pulled my coat collar up and zig-zagged, but she was still there. Everywhere I go, she follows me. She appeared between the eaves of a building and this time I was sure of it; but when I looked there was no one there. Just men in grey coats, walking stiffly and holding umbrellas, despite the fact it was sunny and relatively warm. It's November, so we behave for November, and we shiver in our coats.

I went back to the museum via St. Pauli station, one of the two guarding ogres of the Reeperbahn, the other being the S-bahn at the far end of the long street. All stations are ogres, aren't they? They squat and loom and charge a toll if you want to pass. They roar. They echo. In the lost mists of time, there's even a legend that they puffed smoke.

Ornate lobby. Late deco pillars, the narrow strips of stone piercing the roof as much as holding it up. This time I hung around in the 20th century, hoping to see her between the Beatles buying leather jackets and high-buttoned coats. Air-raid sirens swept me past Hitler's glass stare and then back, back, tumbling towards the other great fire that destroyed much of Hamburg the first time round, centuries ago.

Souvenirs that were a commercial success at the time: remains of wine glasses seared together by the immense heat, looking as though they'd bubbled from the lip of a volcano. Coins fused into each other, their colours green and peacock and violet. Amorphous jet objects. Strangely ominous jagged lumps of matter, the product of a diseased imagination or a late-morning nightmare.

She wasn't there. But I saw her twice on the way home. And she was still in the painting. A gondolier grinned leeringly. I tried to sleep, and I stepped through her dreams.

I finished the painting with less than my usual perfectionism. I just wanted to see the back of it; I hope they still pay me. I made my way to Jan's shop to see if he fancied a few drinks. He looked up from an engraving he was cataloguing and nodded.

'Of course. What's brought this on?' (Usually it's Jan who has to persuade me out.)

'I've got to tell someone,' I said.

'Tell me about what?'

I told him. He laughed. 'Ghosts now, is it?'

'I think so. I see her everywhere.'

'Everywhere?' You can always rely on Jan's precise mind. He laid a ruler on the catalogue, leant back on his stool and winced.

'Street corners. Up and down the Reeperbahn. It's as if she

knows me. I've only met her once, but she smiled as if she recognised me. She knew me.'

'I see. You're working too hard, is all it is. It's happened before.' Jan heard his bell – he must be psychic, I never hear it – and went through the curtain to an overcoated punter browsing through the racks. Pudgy, 50s, grizzly grey, tobacco fingers. His glasses steamed up as the warm air made itself at home on his face.

'Can I help you?'

'Well…' said the man, indicating a 17th century engraving of Priapus. Slight American accent, that he tried to disguise. Why? We like Americans here. Assumed guilt on his ample shoulders?

'I guess I was wondering where the… good stuff is.'

'This is the good stuff,' said Jan.

Ah well. No customers all day, and then the usual. He walked to the counter, enjoying the pitch even though he knew nothing would come of it. 'Many of these come from – you know… the secret museum under the Vatican.' He made his voice inaudible on the last word and just mouthed it. The punter looked at him Americanly.

'And over there – that's the secret wartime stash of you-know-who.'

'No, I don't know who,' said the customer. 'You see,' he explained, 'I want tits and cunts.'

'Oh,' Jan said, affecting sadness. 'Well this,' he spread a hand at his empire, 'is much better than tits and… things. This,' he paused grandly, 'is a pornotheka.'

'A whatica?'

'An antique one.'

Silence. The silence of a traveller, at sea in a land of strangeness.

'Erotica,' Jan explained. 'You saw the sign?'

'Sign? They said any of these shops would sort me out.'

'Try the shops on either side. Or opposite. Any of them, really.'

'Right. Thanks very much.' The man tipped a finger salute to his head and turned. 'No offence,' he said as he reached the door.

'Not here, no.'

Jan as he came back through the curtain: 'They have money, don't they, Americans.'

'So I've heard.'

'A shame really.' We reminisced about how things weren't as good as they were in the old days, as the rain drummed on the skylight.

'Of course, the internet has screwed everything up.'

'Mmm.'

'Where's the excitement, if you've got it on a plate? You need to go and look for it, that's what makes it exciting.'

'I suppose so.'

'No suppose about it. I mean if a woman just stands in front of you on the bus and takes all her clothes off, there and then... it's not exciting, is it?'

'I think I'd find it exciting.'

'No, but you know what I mean.'

I nodded and commiserated. You have to support a friend in his hour of need. The rain rattled more fiercely, joining Jan in his annoyance.

'I don't understand why you gave up painting in the first place,' he said.

Being a murderer, I couldn't answer. I just made more sympathetic noises.

The rain drummed erratically, like Ringo. 'Shall we go out then?'

We had a few rums, but neither of us was really in the mood. I drifted back to the 90s, or was it even the 80s. I was in my old studio six stops out; larger, but not much vibe, no sense of being where the action is. Commissions at one end and what I wanted to do at the other. If I did four hours of commission in the morning, I allowed myself the afternoon to paint what I liked. The discipline; I am nostalgic for it.

But what does it matter now, being a murderer and all that. I had long hair and a moustache; we all thought it was still the 60s, we looked bloody ridiculous actually. I destroyed most of the photos, but apparently people put them up on something called Facebook. I dare not go near it; I couldn't face the horror.

And I can see, as I walk round the flat in my mind, the portraits of Clara that adorn – the word is a cliché now but with Clara they really did adorn, she was adorable – every wall. I painted her from every angle, and stuck the pictures in every available space. Portraits; full-length, clothed, nude, a bit nude, a bit clothed. Full-length; in a hallway, on a beach, in a hammock, on a boat, jumping from a bed, mirrored. Dancing, joking, laughing, drinking. Kissing her own arms, her legs. I shake now to think of it. Obsession would not do it justice. She overwhelmed. She could construct and destroy me in an evening. Seeing her talk to someone else; it was like being ripped open. Smiling, and it wasn't at me; I couldn't cope.

Not that any of this is an excuse. As a murderer, I can't defend myself. (How would that go? I'm sorry, I won't murder her again.) No – there is no starting point; only endless finishing points, all of them the same.

And as Jan got us another rum (why am I drinking this? Why am I even here? Because I'm a murderer and I can't go home) fast-forward, as one does in one's mind on rum, to the last six months, the giant unfinished canvas of Clara's unbelievable face, dominating the studio. Floor to ceiling, a square of beauty to rival Krakow's Rynek, Trafalgar, that square in Vienna. Two hundred, three hundred hours I spent on it. I never finished it, I even thought at the time perhaps I would never finish it. I

would keep reaching for perfection until one or the other of us died. As, indeed, turned out to be the case.

And she came round, that Wednesday afternoon, it snowed, it hailed, and said she hated it. No sign of encouragement; no forgiveness for it being incomplete. Just, 'I hate it.' Well, you know what happened. I don't need to illustrate – ha ha! Sorry. I gave up my career as a result. No excuses. But those hundreds of hours, circling perfection, trying to land on it like a gnat dizzied by a garden; you can understand, perhaps, even if you can't forgive?

Palette knives everywhere; knives from dinner; even the carving knife was to hand. The perils of the open plan kitchen/diner/studio. Artists should never be allowed artists' flats. They don't think about this in Ikea. But there you go, I'm making excuses again.

There was fumbling, I remember that, the brushes dancing and rattling like snare sticks, the pots of turps bouncing and falling to the floor, the sickly smell enveloping the room. Something about a Stanley knife. Something about Clara saying she didn't want to see me again. Something about the giganticness of the painting. The metallic yellow of the knife contrasting with the purples and whey tones of the portrait, and me lunging towards her, sidestepping the painting. It was a stressful week, I'll admit that, as I go over and over those thirty seconds and probably will do for the rest of my life, or for as long as my mind holds out, whichever is longer. I spent so long on that damned painting that at the moment when the knife ripped into flesh and skin gushed blood, I no longer knew which was the real Clara and which was the portrait.

I look out through my studio window, and see steam rise on the wasteland. How lucky I am to have that wasteland there. It was the work of minutes and a few bin liners. If you've visited the Reeperbahn you will know the characters that line its streets. An artist carrying manikin parts in black plastic bin liners and dumping them on the wasteland at dead of night is, if not an everyday occurrence, something most of us have probably seen at some point. So if anyone had seen me, and no one did, there would have been little suspicion.

We're conditioned to think murder is difficult to cover up. It's to stop us doing it, I suppose, and that's not a bad thing, I also suppose. Well. It isn't difficult, if you're a well-regarded local eccentric and your model has disappeared many times before in her life, frequently turning up on a different continent, and whose family hold no interest for her, and for whom the feeling is mutual.

'Look at this.' Jan examined a statue of the Venus of Ephesus. She held up two or three of her breasts in one hand, some of the others dangled, and the rest pointed in various directions. 'Remarkable, isn't it? Like an ancient Mona Lisa.' Jan placed her on the desk. 'Wherever you stand, her breasts follow you round the room.'

'They look rather like eggs.'

'True. In fact there's a theory that – '

'You've got some weird stuff in here.' Stefan picked up a midget with three dicks.

'They were weird people, the ancient Ephesians. It's been here a whole month and no one wants it. Very reasonably priced.'

Stefan nodded.

'I don't suppose you'd like to buy it?'

He shook his head.

'Discount for friends?'

'Sorry.'

They walked to the bar on the corner. 'Look,' said Jan. 'There's another one. I find this lady disturbingly attractive, I have to say.'

Across the road two men in orange jackets pasted a large advert against a crumbling wall. It showed a full-length image of a woman walking down a street, cleverly designed so it looked like a gap in the wall and she was emerging through it. She held a blue and green orb of perfume as if it were the world.

'Oh…' Stefan murmured.

'Don't tell me you haven't noticed her before,' said Jan. 'She's everywhere. Everywhere, she is. Gorgeous, isn't she?'

'Ah.'

They walked down the street. 'I think,' said Stefan as Jan pointed to a magazine hoarding, the woman from the museum again plastered across it – 'that I need to confess something to you.'

A café by the canal. Tower block windows reflected on the water, spiked by the triangles of churches. And Stefan, seeing guillotine diagonals in them, confessed his crime.

Jan thought carefully before speaking. 'This is why you gave up painting?' He sat bolt upright in his seat; analytical, clinical. What do we do next, Stefan could see his eyes asking.

'Of course.' Stefan breathed on his coffee. It's true, that thing they say about the condemned man – that you notice details more thoroughly. The building opposite had a non-symmetric, cuboid wall of glass. It reflected the reflections, subverting them; questioning reality. What was he doing? Confessing? Why was he doing that? Because he could not not.

'What else do you remember about the evening?' Jan asked. 'What did you do with the body?'

Stefan spread his hands above the coffee and examined the twitch in his fingers. 'In the wasteland. It's handy.'

Jan smiled. 'Sorry.'

'I see it every day from the window… you don't have to bury things deep, for them to be gone by morning.'

'No one saw you?'

'I wouldn't be here, if they had.'

Jan nodded towards the waiter and left some coins on the

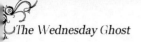

table. 'Come with me,' he said, pulling the mournful Stefan up by his coat collar.

In the cold air their faces changed from blue, to red, to yellow. Ripples from the canal danced across them, changing their expressions like a newborn baby appears to smile, or appears to frown.

'Stefan, I was there,' Jan said. 'Don't you remember?'

He appeared to grimace, appeared to look surprised.

'There was a lot of noise, and I came running up from the shop. Clara was there. She said she was leaving you. You lost the plot.'

'I know, I know. You don't have to remind me.'

'You put the knife through the painting, Stefan. You ripped her face apart.'

'There was blood everywhere…'

'It was paint, Stefan. I helped you clean up.'

Jan took Stefan to the lake and bought him a takeaway brandy. 'It's far too early,' Stefan objected.

'You're very well behaved for a truant murderer,' Jan observed as his friend sipped it reluctantly.

'She drove me crazy…'

'I know.'

Well if it's true… where did Clara go?' Stefan eventually asked.

'The States, I think. You could probably find her on Facebook.'

Stefan shuddered. 'But I buried her on the wasteland…'

Jan shrugged. 'I don't know where you get that idea from. I put you to bed. You were raving. I think you slept for about two days. Clara was pretty sour about it, I seem to recall. She said she had paint on her coat. Said that we were both complete nutters, and left. Didn't even close the door. I cleared up some of the paint, but…'

'I hallucinated it all? I can see myself doing it, I wake up in the night thinking about it – '

Jan shrugged. 'Too much turps, perhaps. At a time of trauma. Your brain has constructed something you could deal with; you couldn't cope with her leaving you, so your mind killed her for you.'

They looked across the lake. The fountain did its sudden shooting up thing, like it had remembered it was supposed to be a fountain and had better get on with it.

'And it was a bloody good painting,' Jan said. 'Don't you remember?'

'I remember… I don't know,' Stefan said. 'I remember everything disappearing from the flat. I thought you moved it all.'

'I did. The slashed painting. That went on the dump, it's true.'

'What do I do now?'

Jan turned and laid a hand on his friend's shoulder. 'You're to go back to painting. You're a great painter. Or, you will be. You shouldn't have stopped.'

I went back to the museum. It seemed safe now. There was no ghost. It was true, I had been seeing her everywhere – she was on the posters. And the smile she gave me, it wasn't because she recognised me; it was because she thought I recognised her. Her image is all over the city; people must come up to her all the time.

I looked at the paintings that spanned the space above the double staircase. Now I know I'm not being haunted, I miss her. But if you see her again, you can talk to her, now you're not a murderer. Marvellous! It seems strange, as I move on to the dark framed portraits, to find oneself not a murderer after all. An ex-murderer; no; not even that.

The paintings present ideas; I develop plans in my head for what I'll do when I get home. A 17th century merchant; fur-lined crags of neck, glistening silver necklace, piles of mouth-watering gold coins on the table and a greyish, unnoticed skull behind. A double portrait, husband and wife, dour, static – look at us, we are important – but the artist evidently too bored even to give their grim expressions any life.

The third is of a family. Gainsborough, or an imitator, the wife in a striking pink dress, dulled to salmon; it could do with a clean. The master in a tricorn hat and hunting breeches, English oaks and elms across their estate in the background, the greens darkened to blue. A springer dog and a small boy, rosy cheeks and pursed mouth, violet eyes cheerful and twinkling. And in the corner of the picture a teenage girl: gawky, nervous and shy but radiant. About seventeen, looking towards the future, wondering what it would hold and quietly excited by the opportunities life might bring. The potential in life; it's dizzying.

It was clearly her. She might have been seven or eight years younger than the woman I saw in the museum, who I saw immortalised in the posters across the city, but there was no doubt about her identity. 'It's her,' I said out loud, and felt myself blush.

The inviting half-smile, looking out to the observer as if in recognition. Who was she? Did she live a long and full life? Did she love? Marry, have children? How old was she when she died? Set me free, she seemed to implore with large hazel eyes, from the claustrophobic, yellowish mist that has fallen upon me over the long, stifling centuries.

'I will,' I murmur. 'I hope you became an old and happy lady.' I step backwards, and have to steady myself against the banister. Time to go, Stefan.

Jan poured the champagne. My first exhibition in five years was of portraits; modern faces, in clothes through history. I painted Jan as a Greek philosopher, holding one of his beloved Venus of Ephesus statues. (Tits everywhere. The *Morgenpost* called it 'sublime'.)

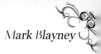

Across the room, a full-length canvas based on one of the figures in *Josef Esterhazy and his Family* dominated the archway, positioned so it looked like the figure was about to step into the room.

Which, after everyone had left and I had drunk too much champagne, she did. She took large lungfuls of air, then kicked the windfall pears that were painted at her feet into brown mush.

'Of course,' she explained as we sat on the scarlet sofa, 'Jan was just suggesting that you hadn't murdered her, because he wanted you to start painting again.'

'Really?'

She nodded.

'So… I did murder her? What?'

'Do you know Caravaggio?'

'Not personally, no. Do you?'

'Do you think he should have been locked up for murder… or should he have spent the next thirty, forty years painting?'

'Well…'

'Imagine the works we would have, if he lived to be an old man.'

'Not the point, is it?'

She looked at me questioningly.

'Is it?'

She put a finger over my lips. I'll worry about it later, I decided. Being a murderer, I felt cautious about kissing her; but she, being unreal, didn't mind.

The Silver Wire

ae Lin sits on the swing, moving slightly with the motion of her foot. I am playing near the sandbox keeping an eye out for the poisonous frogs that spring like lice from the sand. I am not allowed in the sandbox. I am not allowed on the slide. I am not allowed on the Merry-go-Round or the teeter totter. I am not allowed near the mango trees because they give me blisters. I am allowed in the playground but only if I sit still by her feet. I am allowed to play with my ponies, but quietly, and only if I do not draw attention to myself while she is talking to the other nannies.

Bae Lin came with the house, like the whitecar. Daddy says that we have to keep her, we're *obligated*. I hate Bae Lin. She makes me eat fish and her room smells like sweet nuts and spicy stuff, and she tells me that if I'm not good the Aswang will get me and eat me. She says that you never know who will turn out to be an Aswang, but that their eyes are red from not sleeping because at night they turn into black dogs and eat children and corpses.

She likes showing me off to the other nannies. They line us up when our parents are gone and compare us, to see who has the best. The nanny whose kid has the lightest skin wins, which means that Justin always loses, cause he's black. His belly button goes out though, which is really cool. Mine just goes in like everyone else's.

I like this pony. It's the pink one with the butterfly on the side. Its eyes are blue and sparkly like Mommy's ring, the one Bae

Lin takes out of the box when my Mommy is out at work. She's wearing it right now, but it doesn't really fit on her finger so she wears it on her thumb. She likes to show it off to the other nannies.

'Let me tell you a story.' Bae Lin looks bored. That means I'm in trouble. She likes to tell me stories when she is bored and not the good stories, the scary ones about the White Lady and Hukluban, the crone. I know that Huklaban is only one of three, the Death lady, but I had to find out about the good one, Idieale from Tony. Bae Lin only likes me when I'm scared.

'It began in my barrio years ago, when I was a little older than you are now.' Her smile is happy and hard at the same time. 'One day a beautiful woman moved into the empty house near the rice paddies. She was older, middle aged. Her hair was long and shiny, straight and so black it was almost blue. Her skin was pale and flawless. She had lines around her mouth from smiling, and lines around her eyes from laughter, but these only made her beauty greater. Soon, every man, old and young, single and married was looking at her in that special way.

'It was in the harvest time when people were praying to Mary and the hermaphrodite Lakapati to bring the rice in swift and full. The woman, who said her name was Haliya, got along with everyone; old and young, man and woman. I used to see her in the market, selling vegetables and gossiping. She used to give me candy sometimes, or fresh split cane if she had it. She was so charming that she won over even the women whose husbands had looked her way with lust. No one wished her any gaba; no ill will at all.

'Haliya became especially good friends with a young woman named Jasmine. Jasmine had recently been married to a fisherman and she was already showing her pregnancy. The gossip in the barrio was that her pregnancy was the reason for the marriage. Everyone knew that Lito beat her. She and Haliya would talk and gossip for hours, you could hear them from the street.

In the seventh month of Jasmine's pregnancy a strange thing began to happen. Her belly began to shrink. Each morning it would be a little smaller, and a little smaller, and one day, a few days after the baby inside stopped moving, it was gone. At about that time Haliya stopped being so friendly to her, it was nothing much at first, from long talks to short ones, to smiles and nods in the market, to finally a blank look when Jasmine approached her in the street. About a week after they stopped talking Jasmine fell down in the middle of the street with horrible cramps. She crouched in the dust and pushed like a chicken laying an egg. Nothing came out but a handful of dust and some small brittle bones. And that was the end of her pregnancy. She has never had another one. Her woman places are dry.

'All through this Haliya grew even more beautiful, even more friendly and more well liked within the village. She became close with another young woman named Librada. Librada was a widow with two children already. She was not as beautiful as Jasmine, she had worked too hard to be beautiful, but she was intelligent and hard; friendly but not blind. At first she liked Haliya, but as their friendship grew she became aware of the older woman's inability to give a straight answer about anything, not even where she came from or what had happened to her family. She always turned the conversation to present things and never spoke about the past.

'In the eighth month of her pregnancy Librada began to have trouble sleeping. The baby's head was pushing against her bladder and giving her trouble. She kept having to go outside and use the toilet. One night, well after midnight when the moon was moving low against the sky, she saw a strange thing flying. It looked like a large bat trailing a malformed, lumpy tale. As it flew closer she could see that it was the head and shoulders of a woman with bat wings protruding from the neck. Its mouth was lined with razor teeth and its lungs, and stomach, heart and liver were trailing behind it like a tail. Its face was familiar, but she could not place it. It was still too far away for her to see.

'Librada crouched among the bushes and waited for it to pass. Instead it landed on the roof of her hut and began to crawl towards her chimney hole. Librada ran inside as quickly and silently as she could. Her children were still asleep on their mats on the floor, but she could hear it dragging itself along the thatch above her head. It moved like a lizard, made the same rustles and thumps.

'Thinking quickly, Librada grabbed the salt from the jar near the fire and poured it in a circle around her children and stepped into that circle herself. A face appeared in the circle of the smoke hole, backlit and blurred by the setting moon. Its tongue unwound like a thin white hose and began coming towards her, drawn by her scent. When the creature came to the salt circle it recoiled like a cobra. It tried again and again from different angles, but always the white salt stopped it. Towards dawn it tried a final time, but flew off before the rays of light could catch it out.

'In the morning, when her children were in the village school Librada set off to find Balan.

'Balan was a witch. She was old and ugly and she smelled of cat piss and spoilt fish. She was well known for being the wisest woman in the village. Librada had no fear as she made her way to the old one's door.

'Balan greeted the widow as a friend and served her adobo and strong cool tea. Librada told her about the things that had happened in the night. The old woman smiled sadly and nodded her head. Yes, she said, what you saw was the Manananggal, the baby killer, fetus sucker. By day it appears to be a beautiful woman, at night a monster. When darkness comes it must split in two, leaving its legs behind to hunt. What you must do first is identify it in its human form.

'Once a Manananggal marks its prey no one else will do. It will keep coming and keep coming until its tongue is inside you and your baby dust. When you know the woman, you can destroy it. Tonight when it comes after you, you must chop off its tongue. You must not worry; it will not fight you yet. It cannot risk damaging its vital organs. Tomorrow look for the woman with the bleeding mouth. If someone is missing, has packed up and fled then it is gone for good and your problems are over. If not, you must wait until tomorrow night, go into its house and destroy its legs so that when dawn comes the sunlight will turn it into dust. Go now, go home and prepare. Sharpen your knife, tonight you draw blood!

'Librada took the old woman at her word. She avoided the market and spoke to no one, to keep her plans safe and away from gossip. That night when the silver-white thread came down again like a snake from a tree Librada caught it in her hands. It was thick and strong and covered in slime. It writhed and gripped her like a python on a branch. Librada could see the strange, warped face looking down at her shaking with rage and anticipation, lips drawn back exposing its fangs. Librada brought the knife down quick and it shone blue in the moonlight. The thick white tip of the tongue lay writhing and churning in the dirt of the floor spraying old, black blood and clear saliva everywhere. The creature shrieked, loud enough to rattle the flimsy palm-wood walls of her house and wake the children. It flew off clumsily into the clear black night.

'The next day Librada wandered around the market observing the women. At the fruit stand she spotted Haliya surrounded by her usual crowd of jabbering market girls. Haliya greeted librada with a smile, but did not speak a word. Librada had kept her eyes on the mouth of every woman in town and had not seen anyone who spoke with any difficulty at all. She tried baiting Haliya, asking her questions and prodding her to speak. Haliya made no response beyond a nod or a shrug. Librada lost patience, she thought that she knew, but lives were at stake. She needed proof. So she brought her foot down hard on Haliya's big toe. Haliya screamed and her mouth was empty, only the base of her tongue remained, a ragged pink stump; her throat was filled with glistening blood.

'Librada ran. She was worried that since Haliya knew that her secret was out she would not transform but would instead run off to heal and later attack another poor woman in another small village. But she didn't guess the power of the monster's need. That night Librada drew another salt circle around her children and smeared their faces with fresh garlic paste. She prayed three times to the Christian's Blue Virgin. Librada waited, shaking with rage, until her little loves were asleep and then she set out into the night, her machete clutched in her hands.

'Librada made her way to the monster's house, keeping her eye on the sky and her ears open, listening for the shushing sound of leather wings. When she reached the hut (it looked like any other palm-wood thatch) the lights were on and smoke was rising from the chimney-hole in the roof. She could see Haliya's legs abandoned on the floor, shapely middle-aged legs, well-turned and hairless, but of the monster there was no sign. Librada walked in silently, cautiously, her machete raised above her head, but when the monster swooped at her from its place above the door it still managed to catch her by surprise.

'The thing fought with its teeth and nails, slashing at her with its fangs and pummeling her with its powerful arms. Librada stabbed at its torso and slashed its face as the clawed hands clamored towards the baby in her belly. Librada sliced one of its hands off completely at the wrist and its blood blistered her skin like acid. The creature screamed and flailed. Finally, with one well-placed stroke, Librada severed its trailing heart. It fell to the ground with a meaty thud and lay slowly beating out blackish blood onto the packed dirt of the floor.

'The creature fell and clutched at itself with its one remaining claw and Librada fell panting to her knees. Librada fell asleep there beside it, drained by exhaustion, and we found her there in the morning. She had not moved at all.

'The creature was quite dead and its lower half had already rotted, having originally belonged to someone who had died long ago. This kind of monster always finds a use for spare parts. The priest came down from his parish near the base of the mountain. It drenched it in Holy Water, the head and the bottom, and they withered away in bright plumes of smoke.

'A few weeks later Librada gave birth to a boy, perfect in every way. He has glossy black hair and wide almond eyes. She has married a fisherman younger than herself and they left the village together and, as far as I know, they have never come back.'

Bae Lin looks at me and smiles. I don't like it when she smiles like that. 'You know, your Momma's getting pretty big. Soon, you'll have a little brother yourself, either that or your Momma will have a handful of bones.'

When she takes off that ring to make my lunch I will hide it in the back yard. She is too mean to wear it. She doesn't deserve that pretty blue stone.

Towards the Sea

ne-eye Boy saw her first, though no one believed him on account of his missing organ. No one but me. He claimed she was a mermaid, long of limb and tail, with hair like newly spun rope, flaxen and thick, falling over breasts sweet as blancmange, nipples cherry-shiny.

He was wrong; she wasn't like that at all.

'She were sitting on t'rock at left of bay,' he stuttered. The small, mostly disinterested, crowd edged away from the bar as the reek of cockles dispersed into the air. Me? I pushed a jug of beer towards One-eye, leant on the counter and beckoned him over with hooded lids and a flicker of an eyebrow.

'Tell me,' I said, 'was she combing her hair?' knowing full well that wasn't her style.

He shook his head, spittle flying from his slack mouth, and grasped his groin, jiggling the contents as he laughed. Dirty boy with his missing eye and reason, he would never know the tender touch of a woman, other than his mother's.

One-eye told me she stroked her breasts, her nipples peeked between the coils of her hair. 'Knockers,' he called them and I flinched. I asked about her tail, which he said was eel blue, and slimy, as if she'd just come out of the water. It slapped, hard, against the rock and echoed across the bay, the sound swallowed

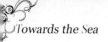

by the roar of the incoming tide. My stomach knotted, and as he spoke of the ropes of her hair I tugged at the skin of my wrists.

She comes.

I lost interest when he spluttered about her fishy smell, repulsed by his vulgarity. 'Cockle-cunt,' he dribbled, as if he knew. Certainly, she smelt of the sea; the tang of iron, strong and unbiddable, fresh. Her perfume shifted, as she did, with each rolling, crashing, lapping lick of the water. I bent down behind the bar, and snatched a cloth from the sink. One-eye hobbled away.

The tide rose and cockling became dangerous if not impossible. Anticipating more customers, I dried pint pots and stacked them next to the pumps. A gust of wind dragged across my neck, and the saloon door slammed. Tom McManus strutted across, the echo of his footsteps reverberating off the sticky walls. He slapped a coin on the bar and flicked his chin, words unnecessary. I was already pulling the pump handle, the muscles in my arms straining, the dark liquid squirting into the pot in explosive bursts. The barrel was almost empty.

Tom grabbed the draught with a grunt and swallowed, the pot not leaving his mouth till it ran dry. He placed the glass down and nodded. I passed him a whisky, single malt, which he knocked back in one.

'Bad shift?' I said.

Tom was a crew leader, well known for the bounty of his hauls. Cocklers feared him, his bullying approach, and the risks he took with the tide.

He shook his head, eyes glazed. Tom liked me, which made me unusual round these parts, and I might have liked him once. Might have. On the other side of the room, One-eye guffawed, and Tom turned his head, sharp, then back again.

'Boy says he saw a mermaid,' I laughed. 'Blonde and buxom, with nipples like cherries and a kiss like heaven.'

Tom caught me in a stare, his violet-blue eyes almost mesmerising against the caramel hue of his weathered skin. Almost. I didn't fall at his feet like other women; I thought that's why he liked me. 'She wasn't like that at all,' he whispered, glancing over his shoulder, 'she was pale, with raven shiny hair and a voice like honey.'

'Tell me,' I said, 'was she singing a love song?' knowing full well that wasn't her style.

Tom told me hers was a song that was hard to remember, hard to distil. Like the tinkling of bells or the plucking of a harp, it was musical but without melody. Like the beating of a drum, it resonated through his body, from his core to the soles of his feet and the top of his skull, but it was without rhythm. It cloaked him like the embrace of a beautiful woman, sweeping over his flesh, its touch like magic. Her legs were long and lean, her arms reached to the cobalt sky and as he buried his face in the triangular patch of hair at the apex of his thighs he felt as if he had reached paradise. He spoke like a man in love, or hypnotised. My breath hitched as he spoke of her snowdrop skin and emerald eyes, her strong fingers, and a mouth that held the promise of another world, deep and dark and dangerous.

Certainly, her voice was spellbinding. Full and wet and tempting, her mouth held many treasures. Her tongue played many a tune on the curves, folds and deep, deep grooves of my body. I ached for her touch and pushed another whisky across the bar, tired of Tom's romancing, longing to be alone with my thoughts once more.

In the cellar I changed the barrel, taking my time, enjoying the solitary darkness, stroking the slits in my neck below each ear. When I returned to the bar, the stragglers from Tom's crew had arrived. Impatient, they banged on the counter. When all but one had been served, I wiped my brow and took a draught of water from the jug reserved for me, the salt biting my lips, seeping into the cracks at the corners of my mouth. Months ago I had loathed the taste, but now I relished the sting and took another gulp.

She returns.

Old-man-Wharton hovered, the last to be served. He brushed my hand as he passed over his coins, then held my fingers, too long, too tight, as he pondered what to order. It didn't bother me the way it did the other girls of the town, the way he did this – pawing young flesh, pushing himself up against girls, and worse. Some said he'd never been right in the head since his wife died. Others said he was a dirty old man who should be locked up. Me? I almost pitied him. Almost.

I pitched forward, elbows resting on the bar, squeezing my breasts together so they pushed over the neckline of my blouse and beckoned him in with my eyes.

'Tom says he saw a siren, out on the bay,' I said, my words little more than breaths. 'Tall and pale with raven hair and a voice like an angel, she stood with her arms raised to the sky.'

Old-man-Wharton gripped me tighter and said, 'She weren't like that at all. She walked across sands, without no clothes, long brown hair falling down her back in tangled knots, like seaweed. Her skin were glossy and brown.'

'Tell me,' I said, 'did she drag her seal skin behind her?' knowing full well that wasn't her style.

Old-man told me she was slim of hip and small in the breast; her hair was so long it pulled on the sand behind her, marking her path from the shore to the rocks. As he drew nearer he realised how short, and young, she was, how brown and wet and playful, and that her long, long hair, was not hair at all, but a pelt. A pelt so soft and tempting he dived into it, allowed it to drape over his shoulders and across his back, warm his flesh and caress his heart. She slipped over and round him, twisting and turning, giggling. Fast and sleek, she was dizzying, with tentacles that coiled about him. Her prisoner, he said, though this was a gaol he would happily live in forever.

Certainly, she was playful, like a child. Full of joy, she was impossible to resist. I liked being bound to her, her captive. Diving and rolling and skimming beneath the surf, she wrapped herself about me, sliding over my earthly flesh, before diving away, weaving between the riptides, fishing nets and clusters of weed.

I feel your pull.

Old-man let go of my wrist and pulled himself up, sighing. 'She were a child, more lass than lady. Just how I like 'em.'

Appalled, I walked away, out of the confines of the bar to the window overlooking the bay. I pressed my palms against the glass, and stared out to sea. Grown high as my knuckles, the webbed flesh between my fingers glowed pink against the midday light.

Hours passed, the tide rose and sidled back once more. The cocklers gathered, taking a drink to sustain them for the hours on the muddy sands. They checked their boots and bundled up in hats and scarfs against an easterly wind, bitter even in summertime. Tom McManus appeared and began shouting instructions, warnings, which most could barely understand and others would not heed.

'Tide's high and dangerous, you mark my words. Fill your buckets, but no risks. We'll want no more drownings round here.'

Murmurs and grunts of agreement rose from the small crowd, and my fists clenched, my nails pressed into my palms till it hurt. The saloon emptied and I went about my work, clearing up, preparing to go home, to my lodgings along the seafront. I was almost done when I smelt her. The tang of metal and salt descended on the bar like fog, mist rose from the floor like sea spray, and subsided as quickly. I looked about, to see if the remaining customers had felt it, seen it, smelt it, as I had. They had not. No one felt her the way I did, no one remembered, or cared. I took my coat from the peg and left without a word.

I heard the cries as I scurried along the promenade, head bent against the wind. The shrieks and wails and screams. I stopped and turned. The horizon was obscured by a mist, and as

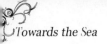

I peered, out came the shadowy figures of the cocklers, running, buckets and rakes abandoned.

'Came from nowhere it did, nowhere,' one cried, as much to the air as me.

'What did?'

'The tide. The tide. Not due for hours, but it came sudden and swift. They didn't stand a chance.' It was a cockler of many decades. She was always furthest from the sea, her crooked legs too tired to walk where pickings were richer.

I took hold of her bony hands; the veins bulging despite the chill of the mist. 'Who?' I said, though I already knew.

'We must get help,' she said.

'Who didn't stand a chance?' I repeated.

'Old-man-Wharton, McManus and One-eye. Out ahead, they were. Miles it seemed. I saw the tide coming in, unexpected, out of time, but coming in all the same. Circling round them, creating an island. There was time for them to get back. We screamed and yelled, but they didn't move. They stood there, like they was hypnotised.'

At the mention of the island, she appeared before me in my mind's eye. A moving image from that terrible day. Held back by two men, I'd watched, as the sea stole up around her, trapping her, on an ever-decreasing patch of sand. The pinky-pale skin of her bare arms gleamed against the sky, her skirt whipped up revealing shapely legs, her blue eyes filled with watery terror. Flame red hair billowed above her head, creating the illusion that she might take off, might fly above the surf. McManus stopped and watched. Behind him, stood Old-man-Wharton and One-eye, the water not even reaching the tops of their wellingtons. They did not even try to save her. I heard her voice, rich and melodious, remembered her words. 'I'm going on ahead, can't stand these two,' she'd jerked her head in the direction of One-eye and Old-man, 'sliming all over me. Give me the creeps, they do. McManus won't care how far I go.'

I'd wanted to go with her but, afraid of the water, I'd lingered behind. After that day, I learnt to swim and never went cockling again. I searched for her, over and over. With each dive I went further, went deeper. But I found nothing, returning to land and loneliness, again and again.

The old cockler shook me. 'Are you alright?'

I nodded, unable to speak.

'We must get help.'

'Hypnotised, you said?'

'They stood there, Tom, One-eye and Old-man-Wharton, then they walked into the sea, as if someone called them, the waves swallowing them up before rolling towards us.'

She is here.

The cockler tugged at my arm, but I ignored her pleas and walked towards the beach, towards the sea, towards my love and the promise of another world, and all that is deep and dark and dangerous.

Storm Dogs

Pen y Cae, October 1949

orothy met him in the Ancient Briton not far from the small village where each of them had ancestors. She had deferred her place at Wellesley for a year in order to see Europe and her maternal grandmother had given her fifty dollars and a camera, a black and silver Leica in a tan leather case. Then she had extracted a promise; Dodo must go to Wales, must take photos of the old farm, the mountain, the church, the gravestones of the Thomas's, the Craddocks, the Vaughns and Dandos.

Everyone stared at her when she entered the pub; she had the sense that she had barged into someone's private living room, though the door had *Public Bar* engraved on its glass. She stood out amongst the local women in her crisp sky-blue slacks, crew-necked sweater and saddle shoes. They seemed mired in the mud and heather, the tree bark and tea stains by the colours of their clothes, all of them in skirts and worn looking winter coats and stout-looking dress shoes. Not that there were any women in the pub at mid day.

He had approached her at once, handsome and smiling, making her feel welcome. He bought her a glass of warm beer. Then he had sung a haunting song in the language of his (and her) people. Everything had stopped in that moment, no one moved, no one touched their drink or spoke or lit the cigarette that dangled from their lips. All eyes were on the black-haired young man as he leaned almost jauntily on his stick and lifted his head and voice to heaven.

When she said it was time for her to go, he walked her outside and asked if he could kiss her. She understood that he had been in the war, that his leg had been damaged by shrapnel or gunshot or mine. She said yes because she was ashamed to say no.

'Marry me!' he said and she laughed and skipped away out of reach.

An hour later she was on the mountain faithfully taking the photos her grandmother had asked for when she fainted. A sheepdog and his master found her; otherwise she would surely have died. She was carried down the mountain on an old enamelled sign that advertised Buckley's beer and woke in an itchy flannel nightgown that stank of old sweat. The farmer's wife was smearing rancid foul smelling grease on her chest and throat. She was in a fever for six days remembering little except for a dreamlike procession of different visitors, a doctor, a nurse, a few small children, the farmer's wife, the farmer himself and his dog, and the young wounded man with the pure singing voice. On the seventh day he came to see her and brought his mother and three sisters to meet her. They congratulated her and held her hand and kissed her. He spoke of their engagement and lifted her left hand to show off the gold and diamond ring she now wore. He had got the ring in France but failed to mention who he had bought it off or the dead hand it had been taken from.

As she lay there alone and exhausted she felt everything was drifting away from her; the water glass with its beaded linen cover, the walls of the room, the train that should have carried her to London, the boat to Calais, the Eiffel tower, Venice with its canals and gondolas, the Coliseum in Rome, the Parthenon, the Aegean sea, the olive groves, the brightly painted fishing boats, the dusty narrow streets that led to open squares with sparkling fountains. All were picture postcards blown out of her hands before she had a chance to post them.

Her marriage to a young Welsh war hero delighted everyone. She was back where she belonged. After the war it was the happy ending they had longed for. To go back on her word, to break her engagement was out of the question.

She married him, hoping for the best, but came to suffer him just as a soldier must suffer his wounds long after the battle had ended. Long after the wound was inflicted.

Dorothy's Journal
The Loire Valley, August 1958

Crossing the bridge our eyes were filled by the imposing presence of the château. Its towers and spires circled and chased by a murder of crows that swooped and cawed. I stopped to take a photograph while Thomas walked on, slowing his pace in deference to my dawdling ways. The weather which had promised fair when we drove towards the town now seemed on the brink of change. While one half of the sky was still blue and filled with high white clouds like those a child would draw, behind the château a great mass seemed to gather and brew, deep lilac grey and gun-metal blue. Heavy and ominous.

Perfect for a moody shot of the 13th century edifice, with the black pen strokes of the winged birds adding drama and interest to the scene.

I took several shots and adjusted the metering to be sure of a good exposure. Thomas was now 20 paces ahead of me and had walked into the shot. He wore his black gabardine coat and dark moleskin trousers and leaned, as he always did, to the right, his cane taking the weight of his body as he limped slowly forward.

With his dark head turned towards the château only his bony wrist and strong hand showed white. I took another shot, this one including him in the composition, but this was no cheery familial snapshot such as a wife should take of her husband, him smiling at the camera with some tourist destination serving as backdrop and proof of their trip, but one which rendered him an ominous stranger, a black-clad cripple; priest, sinner or necromancer. Perfecting the graphic composition as artfully as if it had been sketched by Beardsley or Doré or Peake.

I had loaded the camera with a roll of 36 exposures and the dial showed 14 frames remained, but when I advanced the film it jammed. I increased the pressure with my thumb, but it did not give way. I knew I dare not force it as the film might snap.

'Come on, Dodo! It's going to rain,' Thomas called and as he did I felt the first few drops of rain. One splashed on my hand. Warmish rain that my skin was almost insensible to. I closed the camera's leather case and keeping the strap around my neck tucked it under my raincoat, then holding it securely between my hand and my body began to run after Thomas.

By the time I caught up with him the rain was torrential, Thomas's hair was plastered to his head, and his glasses were washed by a moving film of water. We were still a good distance from the entrance to the château and the winding road that led steeply up to it was lined with small houses of differing age, but there was no shop or café where we might seek shelter.

'Damn it!' Thomas shouted, but I barely heard him so loud, so all consuming was the relentless pounding of the rain. The cobbled street had become a river and we seemed to wade through it as if for the sport of it. In this state, our shoes sodden and waterlogged, our clothes and hair drenched, everything wet through, there would be no château visit, no pleasant lunch on the square, nothing but a miserable retracing of our steps, a return to the small hotel and an afternoon amongst our dripping, steaming clothes and towels.

I was a few paces ahead of him and running blindly with my head bent forward, when a door to my left was abruptly pulled open and a beckoning arm urgently drew me in. I all but fell into the doorway and seconds later Thomas plunged in behind me, bumping against me and making me stagger forward into the room. I heard the door slam shut and then the noise of the storm was muted. It still lashed angrily against the window panes and roof, but it was powerless, a watery demon disarmed.

I sighed with relief and wiped my hand over my face and back over my hair, stemming the tide of liquid that ran down my forehead, into my eyes and poured off my nose and chin. It was only then that I took in the kind stranger who had opened her home to us. She was a tiny, ancient woman with fine white hair scraped back over a bony skull. Her back was hunched and her once ample bosom had sunk to a broad fleshy mound. She wore a shapeless frock that, because of her diminutive size, almost covered her ankles. Her surprising large feet had been pushed into a pair of worn sabots and grey lisle stockings drooped in rolls around her lower legs.

'Merci Madame! Merci!' Thomas said rapidly and with great warmth. She did not reply but nodded and gestured towards the old fashioned black stove that dominated the room. She opened the iron door and poked at the coals rousing them into fierce life, then turned her attention to me and partly by gesturing and partly tugging at one sleeve she encouraged me to take off my coat. There was a wooden airing rack over the stove and she unwound a rope to lower this, then draped my coat and Thomas's over it. Next she pointed at our shoes and from a copper box produced sheets of newspaper which she pushed into our shoes before lining them up on the hearth.

I took my camera from my neck and finding that it was still dry I put it on the large table by the side of the fire.

Our socks and stockings were taken and wrung out over the hearth to sizzle and steam, then they too were draped over the airing rack.

Thomas let out a steady stream of thanks and elaborately formal expressions of flattery and gratitude in perfect though badly accented French. He was in the middle of such a speech when our host began to shoo him away from the fire and towards a very narrow and steep flight of wooden stairs. Up he limped, his naked feet almost soundless on the steps, while his walking stick played a slow tattoo, one, then one, then one. She followed and I heard the floorboards creak overhead, then a door creak and then the shuffle and slap as the old woman descended to turn her attentions to me. I was likewise shooed into another room, that I understood at once was the old woman's bedchamber as there was a metal bedstead painted white and beside it a sturdy three legged stool by which means she must have climbed in and out, for the bed was very high and she was remarkably small. Shrunken by old age and bent by osteoporosis, she was the size of a child of nine or ten. Once more she tugged at my clothes encouraging me to remove them. She was right of course; they were soaked quite through even down to my underwear. While I peeled off my cardigan and blouse, she searched in a tall chiffonier until she found garments she deemed suitable for me and she draped these over the bed. As I stood there naked except for my brassiere and pants, her parting shot was to press a threadbare towel into my hands, then to mime, quite unnecessarily, the vigorous rubbing and tousling movements I should make to dry myself.

I suppose I might have found her manner overbearing, for she did not smile, nor show any expression of warmth, but gratitude and her great age combined with her almost doll like size quite disarmed me. It was as if Thomas and I were two orphans of the storm she had chosen to take under her wing. Or two stray dogs, one of them lame and almost blind, that she had found cowering and half-starved in the street.

I wriggled out of my underwear, then rubbed myself dry and wrapped the towel around my head in a turban. I looked at the clothes she'd laid out for me, eggshell blue camiknickers and a matching suspender belt made from silk with a trim of white lace, seamed stockings and black satin shoes with an ankle strap. Finally there was a lavender grey dress of crepe de chine that fell from the shoulders to the waistband in soft folds, while the skirt, as it had been cut on the bias, skimmed over the hips and fell in flowing airy flutes to just above the knee.

They were none of them garments I would have chosen to put on, being given more to practical skirts or slacks, to cotton blouses and aertex shirts, but once I had them on I could not help but examine my reflection in the looking glass. My skin, it seemed, had done well by its dowsing with rain water and looked soft and translucent. The dress was a very good fit, indeed it might have been made for me.

I rubbed my hair and found that the rain had brought out both the natural wave and a new glossy sheen. If I had ever wished for such a transformation or attempted one I never, in my wildest dreams, could have imagined the creature who now stood before me. I was (and perhaps it was the dim but electrified light that crept through the shutters, the antique glass in the mirror, the curious and transformative strangeness of the day's events) quite beautiful.

I gathered my wet things from the floor and went back into the room where the stove was. There was no sign of either Thomas or the old woman, so I busied myself by hanging my clothes on the rack, then when that was done I began to look with interest at the room itself and all it contained. Like many of the houses near the château this one was of a great age and the room was low ceilinged with roughly hewn smoke-darkened beams that here and there showed the wooden pegs used to drive them together and the marks of the tools that had made them. A great cauldron hung on a chain near the fire and the rafters were here and there festooned with bunches of drying herbs: bay and rosemary and lavender. In one corner a brownish side of bacon hung from a sharp hook and nearby some other object, black and crusted with age, also hung, though whether it was a truffle or dead mouse I could not tell. I only hoped that we would not be invited to eat it.

On the table next to my camera, there was a cracked earthenware bowl containing three hen's eggs. Beside it on a newspaper were six yellow tomatoes and a small cucumber with a skin as warty as a toad's. Then there was a bread board, a long knife with a striated bone handle and the heel of a baguette.

The floor was tiled in deep red and dipped in shallow troughs where many generations of feet had worn it down.

It seemed that time had stood still in this house for three perhaps four centuries. I looked ruefully at my camera and willed it not to be broken, then as there was still no sign of either Thomas or the old woman, I drew up one of the chairs, sat at the table and took the camera out of its case. I tried the lever to advance the film once more but it would not budge, then rather regretting the waste of unexposed film I pressed the button under the camera which released the locking mechanism and began to rewind the film onto the spool in the canister. If I was quick I could reload more film and get a few shots of this unique interior and if I was allowed a number of pictures of our ancient host too.

As a rule once the button is pressed the film winds easily and quickly back into the metal casing, but as I turned the knob I met with more and more resistance until I found I could not move it in either direction at all. Opening the back of the camera would mean ruining any or all of the frames I had taken that day. So unless I could find a darkroom, I would be without the camera for the rest of the trip. If it hadn't been for the frames I had taken of the château with the storm clouds behind and the circling crows and that last one when Thomas had stepped into the frame, I would have sacrificed the one roll of film for the sake of the many I planned to take.

I was agonising over my dilemma when I heard a step and then another on the stair. Slowly and irregularly at first, then it seemed to gather pace and gained the steady rhythm of one step after another, each the perfect echo of the one before and far too spritely I thought for either the old woman or Thomas.

The rain had begun to lose its intensity and now it stopped abruptly, making me as acutely aware of the swelling silence as if my ears had popped.

'Dodo?'

I turned and there was Thomas dressed more or less in the sort of clothes he usually wore, a white shirt, dark trousers, a jacket, but there was something distinctly different about them. The trousers were fuller and had pleats and turn ups, the jacket was far broader and also padded in the shoulder exaggerating his masculine form. His hair like mine seemed altered; it was combed back from the brow and shone as if he had dressed it with hair oil. But strangest of all was that he was standing up straight with his weight evenly distributed on both legs. He still held his cane but in such a way that it seemed a mere affectation, an accessory with no function besides its silver tip and ivory handle.

'Where's the old dear?'

I shrugged.

'And what are you wearing? You look like a…'

I never discovered what I looked like to him at that moment, as the woman suddenly reappeared from the back room carrying a tray.

She fussed silently with three deep bowls, each of them cracked and stained, putting them on the table and laying beside them mismatched soup spoons. From the oven she brought a small crock pot. It was glazed white and crudely painted in blue with rustic scenes that by the costumes of the shepherd and his maid must have been 18th century.

She beckoned us to the table and we sat, catching each other's eye as if to see if it was okay, if we should obey our host and eat with her. Thomas would have been all too aware of my American scruples in regard to hygiene. I tried to avoid looking too closely at the many chips and fissures in the crockery and did not let my mind dwell on the centuries of grime and fragments of food and germs they must contain.

She lifted the lid from the pot and inside we saw a thin yellowish broth, the steam carried to our nostrils a sweet garlicky smell. With a ladle she filled each of our bowls in turn. Thin strands of vermicelli slopped like white worms into the bowls and tiny green flecks floated on the oily surface.

'Bon appetite!' cried Thomas, all false conviviality, then he raised his spoon to his open mouth, clacking the metal against his teeth. The old woman picked up her bowl in both hands and held it by her gnarled fingertips as a diamond is held by the ring's claws.

'Goddamnit,' I thought, narrowing my eyes at my husband. 'I'll show you,' and I picked up my bowl, turning it in my fingers so that my lips should not come into direct contact with any of the chips and I drank. Oh yes, I drank noisily and heartily and the old woman nodded at me in encouragement and ladled more soup into my bowl. I tipped my head back and let the fine threads of pasta slither into my mouth.

You can keep your Nathan's Hot Dogs. Your New York Strip, your Southern Chowder, I thought, I will eat only this. In this simple kitchen. Cooked by Mama.

I looked up and saw that Thomas was staring at me. He had stopped eating and laid aside his spoon. Defiantly I drank the last dregs, put down my bowl and, aware that a film of grease coated my mouth and chin, I drew the back of my hand over it, wiping it clean.

The light in the room suddenly changed, a warm golden glow spreading from the windows and across the floor, making the old woman's face lose its dull grey pallor. Her cheeks seemed fuller, pinker and though still lined by age, she seemed to shed many weary years. She smiled indulgently at me and I melted under her benevolent gaze, held fixedly in her twinkling grey-blue eyes.

Thomas stood up abruptly and began removing his clothes from the drying rack. His cane, I noticed, was abandoned, hooked over the back of his chair. I wondered why he had ever bothered with it; his injured leg had healed long ago.

'They're just about dry,' he said. 'And the sun's come out!'

He made two roughly folded piles of clothing and brought mine to me at the table. I shook my head and barely glanced at them. Angrily he put them on the table, the plain white cotton undergarments uppermost. They were like something a child would wear and I was no longer a child.

'Dodo,' he said. 'It's time we left!'

I looked up at him; he'd run his hand through his hair so that it no longer lay flat and glossy but fell in a short dry-looking fringe over his forehead. He looks like a foreigner, I thought, like one of those Tommy boys from England or worse, those dough boy Yanks.

He rolled his eyes then gathered up his clothes and stomped up the stairs. I listened to the creak of the floorboards overhead, the sounds were interspersed with other noises, the regular tick, tick, tick of the mantle clock, the muted crack and whispered collapse of the coals shifting in the fire.

I sighed and smiled happily at Mama. It was good to be home. She went to the cupboard in the wall by the stove and brought two small glasses and the bottle of eaux-de-vie. She filled the glasses to the brim and we each dipped our heads to take the first sip before the drink was lifted to the lips.

I gave a little shudder at the first swallow as I had always done as a young girl. I closed my eyes and sat back in the chair, running my tongue over my lips savouring the fiery sweetness of the digestif. It was pleasantly warm in the room and peaceful. I dozed off for a couple of minutes, no more, and dreamt that I was a bird. I didn't know what sort of bird I was, but I was soaring on a thermal with my wings outstretched, my feathers stirring and fluttering in the wind. I seemed to have no weight, it was effortless and it was happiness such as I had never known before.

I did not wish to ever leave that dream, but a hand was shaking me awake and there was Thomas, dressed in his own clothes again.

The old woman had moved to an armchair by the fire where she slept, her mouth hanging open slightly, her chin sagging on her chest.

Thomas led me to the door, tugging gently at my hand as I gazed at the old woman and hung back like a recalcitrant child. Then we were outside on the street once more and Thomas slammed the door behind us decisively.

'You look ridiculous, you know,' he said in a hiss. 'Here are your things.' He pushed a brown paper parcel into my arms. 'It goes without saying that you have shocked me. How could you drink that dishwater she served us? I thought you'd have the good sense to pretend like I did. And as for that liquor! My god, you're quite drunk, aren't you?'

He set off up the steep hill towards the entrance to the château again. He was carrying his cane tucked under one arm and striding ahead. I ran a few paces to catch up with him, but my head was reeling, and the shoes I wore might have done justice to walking, but running uphill half drunk in the blazing heat and light of mid-afternoon?

A small truck came rattling round the bend and I saw the driver's eye follow me, turning his head to pucker his lips as he let out a shrill whistle of approval.

Thomas had rounded the bend and by the time I caught up he was entering the carved archway that led into the château. I followed and found myself at the foot of a broad spiral staircase. I paused a moment listening to distant echoing steps going up, further and further away from me. I must have gone up forty or so steps, when I stopped, opened the package, retrieved my walking shoes and slipped them on. My head was clearing; I felt energised and so I began to move faster. The dress brushed against my legs and the rubber soled shoes gave grace and accuracy to my fast moving feet. Up and up I went, stopping once to gaze out of a narrow window to the cobbled courtyard far below where other visitors milled about in pairs and groups. One man stood just below me, a camera aimed upwards, obscuring his face. Where was my camera? Thomas had dragged me away so suddenly I had not even thought of it. I threw myself at the stairs again, running, taking two, then three steps at a time. Surely he would have picked the camera up for me. It had been there on the table near his elbow. He knew what it meant to me!

I reached the top of the stairs. They ended in a circular well in which there was only one door. A wooden door that was banded with black iron and scarred all over from bottom to top with carved signatures, many of which were dated. I saw the year 1668 swing away from my gaze as I pushed the door open. A clear fresh wind hit me, tossing my hair and rippling through my dress. Ahead of me was a narrow walkway that led from one tower to the next. On one side was a crenelated wall, on the other side nothing but a sheer drop. Thomas stood halfway, he had the camera in his hands and was leaning forward slightly from the waist aiming the lens at the courtyard. I watched him for a moment with relief, thankful that he had remembered the camera. Then I realised that any shots he took would ruin my pictures by producing double exposures!

'Thomas!' I called. 'Don't!'

He turned sharply at the sound of my voice and his walking stick, which he had tucked under his arm, clattered onto the walkway, then half rolled, half bounced over the edge. He lunged sideways, his hand clawing helplessly for the cane, then his injured leg buckled and, both arms flailing, he pitched forward over the edge.

There was nothing slow or magnificent about his descent, it was nothing like flying. When he landed there was a noise that I will never forget. A woman screamed, but it seemed very far away. I don't think it was me.

I stood there blinking for a moment, hardly believing what had happened. I could not take it in. I stared at the place where he had stood as if willing what I saw to develop fully just I watched images appear in the developing fluid in the darkroom. Then my eyes went to the ground where his feet had been. There was my camera, the case half open, the neck strap making a looped whorl. It had landed on its back, the delicate glass lens uppermost. Unbroken.

Enter the Petal Throne

t was a place I wasn't unaware of but had never visited, had no reason to. It was not a place I was recommended, nor had I been sent. The frontage was upholstered in what appeared to be red leather, studded with brass nails. It had an uneasy fleshy feel to it, like the blush of freshly beaten skin. The sign was simple, unobtrusive. It read 'The Petal Throne.'

My mother had warned me about such places. Not that she knew about them beyond what she had been told. Not that she could have imagined the places I had actually been. My mother with her blue door, rowan at the gate, all that fierce belief, withered.

The traffic roared in my ears. An old city, brazen enough to forget its own memory. I was not so fortunate.

I stepped over the threshold. Distant music, muffled, out of reach, the promise of lights, dancing but nothing to be seen other than the dim glow that illuminated row upon row of variously coloured liquids, clouded, viscous, odd shapes held within that could have been the slow drift of sediments or objects, misshapen, preserved.

A man stepped forward from a hidden set of stairs, elaborately moustachioed, limbs creped in velvet. He smiled through the whitest of teeth and extended a hand.

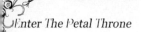

'Gilmartin' he said, mellifluous and faintly haughty. 'My name is Lachlan Gilmartin.

How may I be of service?'

'That depends on the service you provide,' I said. His hand was damp to touch, cool but not weak. Any show of weakness was surely an affectation.

His eyes glinted. 'My dear man, we provide all of them.'

'Then how will I know what I want?'

'To know what we want,' he said. 'Is merely a matter of admitting it to oneself.'

He turned my hand in his. 'There are those charlatans, those mountebanks, who claim that in the pattern of your palm they can tell your future. The best they can provide is justification.' His eyes were amber in the dim light. 'Of course not all of us need such an excuse.'

'I didn't catch your name,' he said.

'I didn't give it.'

He laughed. 'Of course you didn't. A nameless man. How charming. I once had a set of tarot cards that featured a nameless man. I forget what it meant. Something to do with loss or descent, it escapes me.'

'I thought only charlatans claimed to tell the future.'

'Quite so,' he said. 'But the weak have their purpose don't you think?' He held up a finger. 'But none of this is of any use to you. Hieroglyphia,' he called.

'This gentleman requires assistance.'

A figure approached, swathed in blue cloth. I could see only her eyes, a furious green.

'Hieroglyphia?' I asked.

He smiled. 'We have many names here. Only the fortunate may remain nameless for long.'

The woman spoke, asked me to follow, raised her arm as if to beckon me.

'I didn't hear you,' I said.

'She cannot talk as you and I,' said Gilmartin. 'At least not in a form you will be able to understand.'

She led me up a set of stairs. I felt his eyes on my back. greedy, voracious.

A room full of diffuse light with a single chair and a stool in front of it. She motioned me to sit. She sat in front of me, face veiled, her head lowered so that I could no longer see her eyes. She took my hand. She spoke.

I heard words. Some recognised, old words, strange dialects, others I had no knowledge of at all and mixed in amongst it the noises of creatures, clicks, chirps, a purr in her chest. And then where she touched me, embossed on my skin like the faintest of tattoos – a rising flock of aged birds, a book bound in wire, clasped shut. I tried to pull my hand away but could not, from the fast trap of her fingers a mouth arose shouting wordlessly.

'You can't write?' I asked.

Spilled ink, a broken stylus, what appears to be cuneiform mixed in with an Arabic script, jumbled, senseless, blurring into a single blue line.

I looked down at her. 'What has this to do with me?'

Up my arm waves appeared, a familiar sea, the nod of fishing boats in the bay, a boy standing at the sea's edge, casting stones out against the surface.

I covered the image with my hand. The sea washed against it. A nestle of houses appeared around the knuckles, smoke cast itself skywards above distant hills.

I pulled my hand away.

And on my arm fire, blue flames engulfing up past my elbow, houses, villages ablaze, people running, the silence of their screams mouths the gooseflesh of my skin, the spatter pattern of random gunfire. A deer runs through it all, mad, panicked, pursued by dogs which tear it down, choke themselves on its meat.

She raised her green eyes. I said nothing.

I saw her with a knife in her neck. No blood came.

She released her grip.

Lachlan Gilmartin smiled. His teeth glittered like undersea pearls. 'What you saw was... troublesome?'

I shrugged. 'Bad dreams.'

'If only,' said Gilmartin. 'Tell me, did you ever fear consequences?'

'Consequences of what?'

'I knew a woman,' said Gilmartin. 'Who found herself attracted to a certain type of man. And what men they were. Men without fear. Or so they said. Yet so full of fear they could only manifest it in others. Frightening men with names that coiled on her tongue. Butchers all. Imagine a beautiful warlord, hands blackened with the tales of what he has done. All she had was desire without thought of consequence. And there were consequences.'

'Are you asking me some sort of question?'

'I wouldn't be so bold.'

Gilmartin turned to the shadows. 'Quarantina,' he called.

'Another of your many names?'

'Think of it as a joke,' he said. 'But with an element of mocking. Love is a sickness too, don't you think?'

'I don't think.'

'Indulge me,' said Gilmartin. 'The symptoms are the same, a certain physiological hyperactivity, a quickness in breathing, a racing pulse and then that sense that one is not quite oneself, a fever enters the personality, behaviour becomes irrational, overblown. Surely a man such as yourself must recognise the symptoms, that passion even if it is cause rather than effect?'

'Do you think,' I asked. 'That somehow you know me?'

'I know everyone,' said Gilmartin. 'Or at least I can recognise a little of myself in everyone.'

From the darkness behind him a figure appeared, powdered,

coiffured. For an instant she put me in mind of Madame de Stael. Her eyes were wide, her face flushed. I could hear the faint music of Chopin.

'What is this talk of love?' she said. 'Surely the best in life is to love or to be loved.'

'If that is true,' I replied. 'Then you must be among the most womanly of women.'

Her eyebrows raised a little.

Gilmartin laughed. 'My dear fellow, you betray your education. Such delicacy in such a rough form. What are we to do with you?'

Quarantina took my hand lightly in hers. Her fingers were dry as dust. She led me into a room occupied by a single baize covered table, tapping her way with a white cane.

A bottle of green liquid stood upon it, an open smoking flame, a cube of sugar, a slotted spoon cut in the shape of crescents, cabbalistic symbols.

'First, absinthe,' said Quarantina, raising the filigreed spoon. I noticed the colour of her nails, scarlet with an undertone of corrupted umber, glistening like knives.

'Absinthe?' I said.

'Yes,' she said.

'Always.'

'French or Bohemian?'

I pointed to the flame. 'I'd assumed Bohemian.'

'You were correct,' she said. 'This is a place of fire.'

I watched her in the light of the flame, her eyes luminous, blank. I became aware of her breathing, heavy, tubercular, the breathing of port vennels, the raw throats of fishwives, calloused with harbour talk. Her lungs creaked like overworked rope. The spoon tremored in her fingers.

'This is old absinthe,' she said. 'Not that poor liquid that passes itself off under the same name these days.'

'Then I have never tasted it,' I said.

She raised a glass. 'It is wormwood. It is poison.'

She spoke no more, put the glass to her lips, gestured that I should do the same. She poured again, repeated the same ritual, the sugar dissolving into a bubble of liquid, a gall of sweetness on the tongue, matching each other drink for drink.

I was a green boat on a green sea, a state of paralysis in which I could neither speak nor move. Her hands curled around the oars, the blood red of her nails glowing dark as stigmata. She dipped a glass into the ocean, ice cold water into the green liquid, it turning milky, opaque, strange shapes rising like old ghosts.

'The louche,' she cried. 'It is mother's milk. Drink it down.'

She forced it to my lips, the glass grinding against my teeth. I gagged, choking, retched into the bottom of the boat. She pulled me back up. My tongue lolled in my mouth.

'Tell me about your mother.'

She sat in a consulting room, a pen and notepad in her hand. Behind her, occupying the whole wall were Rothko prints, solid walls of maroon, glowering down upon me like corrupted flesh. 'Tell me about your mother,' she repeated.

I tried to clear my head. There was nothing but fire, fire in the darkness as if it was a breathed presence and a roaring, a black roaring that filled my vision. Then a boy, a boy at the sea's edge, banging on a drum. All around him gulls rose, a cloud of panicked wings, vortices of feather and beak until all that remained was the boy and the beach, his hand paused above the drum. The sky held its breath waiting for what he did next.

And here I am. An alloyed landscape, a train yard, a single set of black rails to the horizon. Metal groaned around me, the mesh of giant cogs, forged iron, rust-red. It moved in a slop of grease dripping, forming ink pools on the ground. I struggled forward, barely able to move my legs. Steam vents purged foul smelling vapour, condensing in black streams upon my skin.

There was a hammering, the glow and hiss of furnaces. I had no idea where I was and then just as suddenly a sound, the slide of a bolt, the familiarity of a chambered bullet. I remembered everything. I became a blade.

I sucked the air back into my lungs, felt my face wet with tears. I jumped from my chair reaching for some form of defence, my arms flailing.

She did not move. 'A bad dream,' she said and lit a cigarette.

'And you,' I asked. 'What did you see?'

She tapped a carmined nail against the rigid surface of her eye. 'I see nothing at all.'

I staggered towards the door. 'I have to leave.'

'If you do,' she said. 'Misfortune will surely follow.'

I looked back to the green bottle on the table. 'Then let it.'

I walked back into the shop. Old tango music was playing softly, songs of broken hearts, stolen loves, crimes of passion. Lachlan Gilmartin was engaged in conversation with a man dressed in the manner of a gaucho, a pair of bolas swinging lazily at his hip. He could have doubled for Valentino.

Gilmartin turned. 'Ah, my friend, you have returned. We were just discussing the parallels in the lives of Carlos Gardel and Robert Johnson.'

He gestured vaguely into the air. 'That song you heard when you returned – *Yo no se que me han hecho tus ojos*. One of Gardel's more famous.' He continued. 'Gardel had the nickname *el mago*, the magician, an implication at the very least of the supernatural, and Robert Johnson famously traded his soul for music. Perhaps you have an opinion?'

'None I'd care to think of at this moment.'

Gilmartin looked concerned. 'I trust your experience here wasn't unfavourable.'

'Unexpected.' I said.

'And you say it with such certainty,' said Gilmartin.

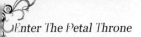

I look to the exit. 'I have to leave now.'

Gilmartin shrugged. 'What makes you think there is anything out there for you?'

'I have to go.'

'As you wish,' said Gilmartin. 'The appearance of choice is only the manner in which the inevitable goads the present.'

'I have to go.' I repeated.

'Then we will expect to see you again soon.'

'I don't think so,' I said.

Lachlan Gilmartin smiled. 'You think you have a choice?'

I pushed through the exit and into the street. An astringent shriek of sunlight poured into my eyes. The air shivered and I gagged at the verdant tingle of my tongue. All around the flutter as of wings, pushing me downward, the fish bone choke of feathers in my throat. I felt myself begin to sink to my knees. The world was a whirlwind around me.

I turned back. I re-entered and gently closed the door behind me.

Singing a New Song

n the third night of Guy's posting to 'Wipers', the bully beef makes him sick. Bile rises from his gut, leaches into the base of his throat. He swallows; he can feel her blood, barbed on his tongue. The Countess, the castle; his travels are a fairy-tale woven from enchanted cobwebs. It's hard to imagine a time before this, and curious to contemplate beauty here, almost wicked.

Sid trades his shaving mirror with Guy on agreement that he'll surrender a pair of dry socks. Trench foot is much on the men's minds.

Guy accepts the mirror with muttered thanks. He settles in a funk hole and draws down the cover, though for once it isn't raining. He breathes in earth stink and rotting flesh before fumbling for his matches. He strikes. He doesn't see his reflection right off – a trick of the dead air, no doubt.

The image evolves as if conscripted into being. His face is a porcelain mask, his eyes stare in an offensive of self-awareness.

'Tsss.' Air escapes through breaches in his teeth. The flame licks his skin; he drops the match.

*

Guy draws his laces tight.

Sid smears whale grease over his feet and slips on the socks. He pauses and contemplates Guy. 'Do you want to lose a foot, a leg?'

Guy looks off, other things occupy his mind.

'Suit yourself.' Sid thrusts his foot into a boot.

An explosion booms: it's close. Morsels of earth trickle from the corrugated seams of the dugout. The punch and zing of bullets follow.

Sid's gaze shifts from door to ceiling; the whites of his eyes glow. 'You young men are all the same. I know. Believed I was invincible when I fought at the Western Transvaal – signed up as a boy, returned a man. Now this: "War to end all wars".' He smiles, a bitter, private smile that seems to invite destruction.

Guy stands and stamps his feet, imprinting the ground. He huffs across his fingers; his breath fogs the air. He needs to get out of this lair, infected with shit and urine, sick and blood. He licks his lips.

Of all the men selected for the wiring party, he was the only one who didn't react.

Sid sniffs and wipes his nose with the back of his hand. 'You ready for this – this jaunt across No Man's Land?'

Guy feels his lips spread as if to shape a smile. No Man's Land: a place for no man.

'Are you brave or stupid?' Sid frowns. 'In another month, the weather'll be with us, and then the show really begins. You won't find it so amusing then.'

Guy shifts to the entrance and tries to suck up unsoiled air, drawing it into his lungs.

Sid turns his jacket inside out, lights a match, and runs the flame along one seam. 'Got the bastards.' He waves the life out of the match before it sears his skin. 'I'd offer to do yours,' he says. 'But they don't bother you, do they?'

Guy shrugs as if in mockery of the men whose shoulders jolt and shudder. He won't remove his jacket and expose the vacant seams.

Outside the firing lulls; a blackbird starts to sing in a repetitive trumpet: two notes long and low; two short and high.

After ten minutes, Sid swears. 'Smug critter trots out the tune, over and over, as if in ridicule: *I'm free, you're trapped* – I swear that's what the bugger sings – aimed my rifle at it more than once.' Sid continues with his mini massacre. 'Never had the heart to pull the trigger. The other lads like to hear it, but I wish it'd change its bloody tune.'

Guy stares at the trench wall opposite; a rat scrambles without fear over the top. 'Perhaps it can't,' he says.

*

They inch out in the mouldering light. They wedge pickets into the earth with cloth-bound mallets.

'Keep focused. Strike again, not so hasty,' Sid tells a new recruit, voice low and assured.

Guy has a soundless tread. He doesn't fumble with the equipment; he's quick, efficient, machine-precise. He doesn't struggle to negotiate his way in the dark. Sid watches him with admiration and something else – fear, perhaps?

Guy's hands are chalk-rock white and just as steady. Sid and Guy unravel the apron and complete the next section as fast as the squelch of mud will allow.

There's a hiss and a flood of light. The sun's switched on.

As if hypnotised to pose as a statue, Sid waits with screwed up eyes. A thud and he's knocked sideways. His limbs tangle in the apron.

Guy is transfixed. He'd heard stories of light-shell rockets. Dusk is displaced to facsimile day. He blinks, adjusting to its harmless brilliance. Every man from his party is cowered in deformed prayer, as if seeking salvation from the mud.

The strike, when it comes, is a punch to his gut. Face in the sludge, he's unable to discern where the earth ends and his blood begins. Blood, he can smell it. He bites on his lip to stop from screaming. He wills his throat to silence, his limbs to rigidity. Part of him wants to laugh; the dead posing as the dead.

Light, artificial and natural, terminates. In the trench on both sides men shuffle and mumble in contrast to the churchyard hush of day.

Casualties, able to move, emerge as if surmounting graves. Guy sees them, and so do the German snipers; bullets hail no man's land. Figures fall, retreat to crud.

Sid's breaths beset Guy's ears. The air is comatose.

Better Sid doesn't wake, but he stirs and moans. His voice: a thin reed, gurgles, 'Hey, Peterson, Mathews, anyone. You out there? Guy. You're not dead, are you? Guy.'

Guy's own injury dulled to nothing within minutes. When he poked his fingers into his ruptured greatcoat, he discovered unbroken skin. Anyone else would call it a miracle. Hunger gnaws to the core of his bones.

Shut up, Sid, please. Shut up.

There are mutterings from the other side and an abrasive laugh.

Sid starts up again. 'Lads, come and get me. Don't leave me. Someone, anyone. Are you out there? Guy.'

As if in reply, there's the suction of boots and a shadow picks its way closer. In the other direction, a click and more muttered voices. No laughter this time. The zip of bullets: one, two. The shadow stops, gasps and falls.

'No. You bastards.' Sid's voice is impossibly high. His breath follows, rough and fast. 'Guy, please. I promise I won't moan about that bird or anything anymore, please.' Words stutter,

'Send another. You're there, aren't you? Guy. Those bastards.' He pauses. A moan, could be a sob, broken by words. 'Just shoot me…don't leave me…don't…not to them, no. Not the rats.'

Put him out of his misery, it's the humane thing to do. Guy's mind clunks these thoughts like a cog and wheel.

But a different voice grinds with gathering insistence; if they leave him, Guy's weeks of restraint can be reasonably fed. The smell of blood pervades Guy's airways and catches in the base of his throat.

*

Just before dawn, Guy skulks towards the scratch of Sid's voice.

An act of mercy, he tells himself. But compassion has little to do with the grip of hunger that has him pinioned in its jaws.

Sid stops calling for him or anyone else.

As the day revives, Guy's flesh starts to smoke; he wills the plume to a wisp. Lost in steaming mud, he's just another casualty.

At dusk he stirs to life.

He's right up close to the watchman before he whispers, 'It's me – Guy.'

The soldier starts but recognises him. 'Get in.'

An officer and two older men evaluate him. The officer, young and pale, stares wordlessly. One of the soldier's foreheads is gouged with a scar. The other has a round face and kind eyes, but he's frowning. 'Every man in your party fell. How are you untouched?' His eyes rove the greatcoat with its punctures and dried blood.

The officer swallows. 'The wire?' he says.

Guy stares at his boots. 'Not secured, Sir.' When he clawed at Sid's body, the wire was torn, leaving a spiked-tooth yawn.

'Christ,' the soldier says.

The other one rubs his scar philosophically. 'Just a jammy bastard, aren't you?' He touches Guy as if he can extort some luck.

The round-faced soldier shakes his head and shifts aside.

*

It's the same the next day and the next, sometimes Guy catches a look as he lights up another man's cigarette. They sense his difference. Whilst they battle with reams of mud and the stink of festering wounds, he has other horrors to conquer.

Guy is no longer a part of their troop.

He thinks of the legacy the Countess left: obsession with humankind and a hunger for blood. But he yearns to be human, even in the filth of a trench.

He cuts his nails, which grow to claws each evening. The sun which scorched her, and every Nosferatu throughout time, causes him only a sizzle as it nurtures a new day.

Some of the men, the more observant, call him 'Smoky', but it's said with camaraderie and a slap on the back. Others look askance, as if he's a dark spirit, but returned for what purpose?

In the dugouts the rat population decreases when Guy's around. The men do not wonder at it; they are too tired for that. They are grateful for small mercies in a place where sanity has turned madman and wields a bayonet.

Many times, day or night, Guy lies, eyes open. He listens to the roll of tins above the trenches as rodents feed on human dregs.

Or sometimes when the shelling stops, he hears the birdsong.

He revisits the fantasy of weaving his bicycle in and out of the fire-bays and traverses, over the duckboards, cutting through slush and bone as if man's machines could defy death. If only he could pedal fast enough, time might slow; it is a dream he has. But there's not much space for dreams here, and he never thinks on it for long.

*

On the fourth week of Guy's third stint, a new recruit joins. He reminds Guy of his former self when untainted by her blood. But in this place innocence will save no one.

The boy curls in a corner and his body shakes as if sub-zero winter has descended. An older recruit mutters in his sleep, but otherwise the men do not notice this new arrival.

Guy shifts closer. 'First time on the front line?'

The boy jumps, eyes, shell holes beneath a metal helmet. He nods; his Adam's apple jerks like a head bobbing above the parapet.

'Here,' Guy delves for his flask that contains the ration of rum he will not drink.

The boy accepts it, takes a gulp and coughs. His eyes turn glassy.

Guy smells his fear. 'I'm Guy. What's your name?'

'Billy – thanks.' He offers the flask back.

'Keep it,' Guy says.

The boy's breathing steadies. 'How long have you been here?'

'Day twenty-four,' Guy says.

'They said eight days maximum on the frontline, four days in reserve and four of rest. Oh God, twenty-four days.'

Guy shrugs. 'There aren't enough men to keep to those schedules.'

'Oh God.' Billy hugs his knees and rocks back and forth.

God isn't listening, Guy thinks. Here is your world of science, your world of progress. And yet something stirs within him. 'The fritz are rotten shots.'

'Are they?' Billy stops rocking and looks hopeful.

'Bloody awful.' He grins.

The boy is drawn to him. Guy has this power now.

'You'll be back in reserve before you know it.'

'I signed up,' Billy says. 'Can you believe that?'

'I'll believe almost anything these days.'

'I wanted to do my bit, be a hero.'

'There are no heroes anymore,' Guy says. 'Just chaps trying to get a job done.' These are Sid's words, spewing from his lips.

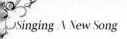

Billy shivers. He takes another sip from the flask and they slip into silence.

*

On the third whistle, they trample the sandbags. Billy doesn't move and so Guy shoves him. If he stays he'll be shot by one of his own. A few yards before they reach the breach point, they see the wire hasn't been cut. Billy stares mouth agape. Gunfire. He staggers and falls. Guy dives on his belly beside him.

'Been shot, shot.'

'Stay still,' Guy says.

Explosions greet their attack. Chaos. The boy's sobs are lost. Later perhaps, he'll have to be silenced.

'I've a letter…see it gets posted? Don't want Mum…Mum to think…want her to be…to be proud.'

'You're not going to die,' Guy says.

'Promise me…promise you'll get it to her.'

'If necessary, I'll see it gets sent.'

Billy bares his teeth, perhaps a smile, perhaps in defence of the pain. The slush around him turns from brown to claret.

Guy pulls a field dressing from his kitbag, rips Billy's jacket open and binds his chest and shoulder. The boy's breath comes in fits and gasps. Guy works rapidly, turning his face away, forcing his need aside.

He looks back, not so far. He waits for Billy's breathing to settle. He lurches to his feet, hooks his arms beneath the boy's armpits. Guy heaves; Billy screams: banshee, barely human.

The boy is lodged like wheels in clay mud. In his mind's eye Guy sees spokes spinning, racing and flying free.

But a tune blossoms in his gut.

This bird will sing a new song.

He is no more monster than the men snarling, shooting and stabbing.

He leans towards Billy, who swallows as if he will speak.

Guy draws closer. He'll keep alive the myth, forged from ancient tongues, now retold as black and white moving pictures of terror. He will find a fresh voice.

He bends, bites into his own wrist and presses the wound to Billy's lips.

The shadow of absolute evil is no longer the fear. Good or bad depends upon which side of the parapet your head appears. The world is a shifting fog of boundaries, like the sky across the Western Front: a bruise.

Mia

o-one else was going to help. I could see that. She was with this bloke at the back of the room, by the door to the toilets. He had her pressed up against the wall, leaning over her, and as I walked past I could see he had hold of her arm, that he was shouting at her. I could see his jaw working, the tendons straining in his neck as he screamed into her face, and she's tiny, she looks all of fourteen years old as he's spitting abuse at her. He was as mad as hell and she was just standing there, taking it.

I couldn't hear what he was saying. The pub was crowded and the music was too loud. Too hot, too loud, too busy for anyone to care. He took a step back and there was something about the way he moved, the set of his spine, made me think he was going to hit her and that's not on is it? So I stepped in.

'Is everything okay?'

I could see Lucy standing by the bar, scanning the room, a glass of wine in one hand, a pint in the other.

'Are you alright?'

It was stupid, really, none of my business after all, and he was a big man. He looked like he might have wanted to make something of it for a minute, but then he let go of her. He let go and wiped his hand on the front of his shirt, slow and deliberate, never taking his eyes off her. He bent down and whispered in her ear, then pushed past me and was gone.

'Are you alright?' I asked again and she nodded, licked her lips, smiled.

She was thin – skinny thin – and pale with smoky, vacant eyes. 'Right.'

And I turned to walk away, only she grabbed hold of me, cheap bangles jangling on her wrists. Her hands were clammy and her ragged nails were painted purple.

'Thanks.'

Her voice was low, soft; I had to lean in close to hear her. Her eyes were blue I could see now, heavy with black eyeliner and smeared with glittering green eye shadow. She blinked slowly and looked at me, waiting. I was close enough to see the goose bumps puckering the skin on her throat, close enough to smell her perfume, honeysuckle sweet. One tooth was chipped, I noticed, and I wondered if he'd hit her. I wondered if he'd hit her before and if she'd stayed with him anyway. I could taste blood in my mouth.

'Will you be okay?'

'I can't go home now,' she said, almost as if it was my fault.

The thing is Lucy and me – it's not like she's my girlfriend.

I looked down at her. She was trembling. He must have scared her more than she was letting on. I looked back at the bar, but I couldn't see Lucy anywhere.

'I can't,' she said, gripping my wrist hard enough to bruise.

And she's not my type, she's really not. But it was hot in there and I was a bit pissed and there was something about the look of her, about that slow, famished look she had.

'What's your name?' I asked.

Mia.

I was properly drunk by the time we got back to the house. We went to another pub which was noisy and full, and another which was dark and cheap and stank of backed up drains and piss.

I remember flicking the hall light on and her standing there. There was something…

She looked so fragile; the light seemed to shine right through her. You can stay here, I wanted to say. Sleep on the sofa. That's what I meant to say. I didn't bring her back just to…

She reached up and switched off the light and in the sudden darkness all I could see were those empty eyes, gleaming. I reached out and pulled her to me and her mouth was hot and wet, and her teeth were sharp, and the taste of her was –

Intoxicating.

That's not what I'd meant. I didn't bring her back just to – I didn't.

Her mouth and her skin and her breath. Muscle and skin and bone. And she wasn't fragile. Not at all.

That was Saturday. And today is…

I don't know.

We stay in my room most of the time, although I think she's been downstairs. I think I've heard her in Simon's room and Alex's too. We keep the curtains closed and the lights low. She sleeps a lot. We sleep a lot, I think.

I remember standing in the hall.

'Come in then,' I said.

And she smiled and came in and I turned on the light and it was bright – too bright –

For a moment there was something about her. I could see – she dyes her hair and paints her face, of course she does – but for a moment, I could see.

Her.

I saw what was underneath, what is underneath. Hidden. Ancient. Hungry.

I dream about it, I think. But then I wake up and she's there and I forget. For a while.

She's asleep now. Next to me.

Naked. Cold.

I opened the door and she stood back, suddenly uncertain, afraid.

'Come in,' I said and she smiled.

They were arguing in the pub, he'd pushed her up against the wall, and sometimes I wonder what the quarrel was about. I try to remember what he said to her before he walked away.

...and don't come back.

The way he wiped his hand. The way she grabbed at mine. But I can't remember what he said, not for sure. I can't remember what I saw, in that moment when I flicked on the light.

I could try now. There's a lamp by the bed. I could look.

But then she stirs and shifts, rolling towards me. She opens her eyes and she smiles.

Her red lips.

Her white teeth.

I can taste blood in my mouth.

The Office Block

ight held a black, fingerless grip on the town, its glutting darkness punctured only by the dim light of the street lamps. Carrying a plate of stale hot-cross buns, Mr. Owen climbed the stairs to bed, his eyelids broiled by the stye-reddened itch of insomnia. He could not know for sure, but he felt as if he was the only person in the town whose body still belonged to yesterday. Everyone else, it seemed, was already asleep.

His heavy limbs rested at the edge of his bed, Mr. Owen waited for the thick coating of butter to soak itself into the spiced buns. The room was dank, despite having been damp-proofed by the landlord just a few weeks earlier, and fresh specks of black mould had begun to steal their way across the white ceiling. Placing the plate on the floor, he switched on the electric heater and began to read – the glow of the heater's halogen lamps providing enough light to see the colour supplement of last Sunday's paper.

Mr. Owen's sleepless nights had a distinct whiff of the temporal loop. At 2am, a second supper was toasted, and taken upstairs to be eaten in bed. Hot-cross buns, English muffins, crumpets – whatever bread-based product had been reduced to clear at the supermarket on the way home from work. Once in bed, he would flick through the pictures and light articles of uninteresting magazines – his mind too drained to engage with

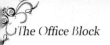

anything of substance – until the watery-grey wash of early morning told him it was time to brush his teeth and put on his suit. He never closed the curtains, he saw no point – he had as much chance of getting to sleep with them open.

His eyes resting on a photo-page of ugly, expensive furniture, Mr. Owen picked up a bun from the plate on the floor. The sickly yellow excess of unmelted, store-brand butter pushed itself into the gaps between his teeth. He hadn't toasted them long enough. Fumbling for the bottle of water at his bedside, he dropped the half-eaten bun to the floor, its cloying milkiness too much for his tired stomach to take. It was a waste, but it didn't matter – he ate at this time of night to quell boredom, not hunger. Wiping a dribble of old tap water from his chin, he switched off the electric heater and fell back onto his bed. The room cooled, as the ghosts of the night streamed through the cracked window frame to seize its dark corners.

Across the street stood a disused office block, a chunk of grey brick hugged by seven rows of single-glazed glass. The last company had moved out over a year ago, and initially there had been talk of 'luxury' apartments, but now the building seemed fated to be slowly demolished by disuse. At half-past two each morning the lights came on, illuminating the long corridor-like office space. Erratic formations of empty brown desks collected themselves upon tiled-carpet, extension leads for now-absent computers coiled around their wooden legs. A few chairs had been left behind too, moth-bitten and bent out of shape, but all electrical equipment and stationery had accompanied the business to its new premises across town. There was nothing left worth breaking in for, so it was strange that the security timer had been left on to ward off potential looters for so long. It all seemed such a waste.

*

'I'm afraid I'm going to have to discontinue your prescription, Mr. Owen.'

He hadn't been listening. The doctor's office was too warm, and he hadn't had a chance to take off his coat on the way in.

'You see, you've been on these tablets for almost eighteen months now, and we've seen no change. I'm sorry, but my hands are tied.'

Mr. Owen nodded. The doctor was a locum, a short man with unkempt white hair and a Bart Simpson tie. His skin tone suggested roots on the Indian subcontinent, but his accent spoke of a childhood elsewhere. Mr. Owen stood up, extending his hand. He would be glad to get back out into the January dusk.

The lamp behind the doctor illuminated his round head, making the thin fuzz on his earlobes look like strips of mislaid sellotape, 'Have you considered natural medicine, Mr. Owen? Let me just find you a leaflet.'

The route home from the doctor's surgery always seemed to take forever, snaking past rows upon rows of terraced homes with cracked roof tiles and thick curtains. Mr. Owen had bought an all-day ticket that morning, but there were no buses in sight. He was off-route – best to just keep moving forward.

Committing himself to sweat patches, he tackled the gradual incline that led from the centre of town to his house. The dark office block towered above it all, surveying its domain. Mr. Owen knew that it wasn't possible, but he couldn't help but feel that it was watching him, devoting at least one of its thin glass eyes to his lonely journey from foot to brow. The words of the locum doctor slowly began to sink in. Eighteen months. No change.

Guiding him through streets he barely knew, the office block grew larger with each step he took towards it. Mr. Owen felt the furthest from sleep he had ever been.

*

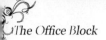

At work the next day, he caught himself staring out the window more often than usual. The previous night had been tough. Of course, every night was a sleepless one, but he hadn't been that restless since this whole thing began. His temples bloated under the pressure of a thousand unfinished thoughts. Too agitated to concentrate on the spreadsheet before him, he tilted his screen away from his neighbour to check the online auctions he was tracking. Expired vouchers, mystery boxes, worn socks. As items for sale, they all fell foul of the website's terms and conditions, and would be taken down long before the auction could reach conclusion. Mr. Owen found that following the narrative of each auction – counting the days before the website noticed the seller's breaking of their rules – passed the time in a way that was not too troubling for his worn mind. He had no desire to bid on any of these items, although the mystery boxes did intrigue him. Most, if not all, would contain nothing of real interest – the contents of a forgotten kitchen drawer, perhaps, or the dregs of a successful boot sale. Things that not even the charity shop would want. But there was no way of knowing for sure, not without opening one yourself.

Trudging home up the hill, Mr. Owen felt the sting of carpet burns on the soles of his feet. He could not spend another night pacing around his room. His sanity could not take it. He filled his evening with monotonous tasks and then, when night came, lay on his bed and counted the stars.

One hundred and ninety seven. One hundred and ninety eight. One hundred and ninety nine.

The leaflet the locum had given him, now dampened by the grease of buttery fingers, had almost convinced him of the benefits of an alternative path. Then, at its end, a price list: 'buy four sessions and get your fifth session free.'

Three hundred and twenty. Three hundred and twenty one. Three hundred and twenty two.

The stars seemed brighter than they should be, outshining

the encroaching glare of the town's layer of light pollution. Mr. Owen thought about buying a telescope, learning how to pick out the asterisms.

Five hundred and sixty four. Five hundred and sixty five. Five hundred and sixty six.

Distracted by thought processes, his eyelids grew heavy. Seconds became lost, some stars went uncounted. Mr. Owen felt a numbness spreading from his ankles. It was finally here.

Light. Filling each corner of the room, dissolving shadows. Mr. Owen awoke from his almost-slumber. It was 2.30.

Across the street, the office block grinned through seven sets of fluorescent teeth.

Returning home the next evening, Mr. Owen paused at his front gate. The office block, stained by rainwater, loomed through the mist. It interrogated him, posing questions without words. On his way to work that morning he had not been able to shake the image of it from his mind, its silent laughter echoing through his skull like footsteps on wrought iron.

Something had to be done.

He had not known what that something was until a clenched fist had smashed into the table in front of him at the end of iteration meeting that afternoon.

'Jesus Christ Owen! Did you hear a word I just said?'

He hadn't heard a word, not one. His line manager's head pulsed like an over-boiled kidney bean. The eyes of the room were on him. Thinking quickly, he plucked a stock phrase from the recycled air.

'I feel that there's definite room for more "light-bulb-thinking" at this company.'

Entering his living room, Mr. Owen peeled the bag-for-life from his underarm crook, allowing its contents to fall through the split onto the safety of the soft carpet below. Unfastening his trouser clasp, he sat down on the sofa to examine his haul. The boy at the shop had been very helpful, racing off down the aisles to gather everything on the list. He probably should have tipped him. The well-worn bag had broken as he boarded the packed 27A. The whole world sniggered. It was the type of event that would normally have haunted Mr. Owen for days; an acute chagrin that bores itself into the mind, returning its victim to the point of embarrassment at every opportunity it can find. But today, there was no room for deviation of thought. As the colour drained from the sky outside his window, the hour-long slots of late night television provided a countdown. Tonight, his second supper would go untoasted. When the channel switched to the stream of 24-hour news, Mr. Owen knew it was time.

Though the wind did its best to deter him, breaking in actually proved to be easier than feared. He could not find any security cameras to blind with cheap spray paint, and the door had opened with the slightest of persuasive whispers from the still-shiny crowbar.

No alarm – he needn't have waited until the rest of the town was asleep.

Inside, the moonlight moved with Mr. Owen, guiding him from the building's entrance to the row of elevator doors on the back wall. Running on autopilot, he pressed the button to call one. A low groan accompanied the opening of the doors, the inside of the elevator lit only by a low-wattage safety bulb. His own silhouetted reflection in the elevator mirror stole a breath from his lungs.

The building knew what he was about to do, Mr. Owen could tell that much. It watched him round corners, listened to his footsteps. So why wasn't it putting up a fight? He had been foolish enough to use the elevator – it would have been so easy to trap him between floors, watch on as desperation devoured him from the inside out. But the office block welcomed him in an almost comfortable silence, not even allowing the rats or the wind to suggest other presences on the floors above him. It wanted this, he thought, perhaps even more than him.

He tackled each floor in almost ritualistic fashion. There was no need to rush. The wielding of the hammer was therapeutic; each light bulb lifting a little of the sleepless weight from his shoulders. By the time he reached the seventh floor, adrenaline was slowly giving way to a feeling of warm content, a comforting itch in his elbows and knees that suggested sleep was finally on its way.

Mr. Owen made his way down the stairs from the seventh floor, only stopping to smash the occasional strip light. Reaching the bottom, he checked his watch. 2.27. He had wanted to be back at his bedroom window by half-past two, but it didn't matter – he could watch the lights not coming on tomorrow night. That was, if he could stay awake for it. Throwing open the fire-door to the lobby, Mr. Owen stopped. Just two light bulbs remained, hanging above its centre. He took them both out with one swing.

Pausing to catch his breath, Mr. Owen felt the office block exhale. 2.29. It was done. Light from the street-lamps cast an orange path between the darkened walls of the reception area, a ceremonial carpet leading from the glass entryway to the company emblem on the back wall. As if making a grand entrance at a benefit dinner, Mr. Owen walked slowly down it, his tired head held high.

A light came on.

On the wall behind the reception desk, hidden beneath a plastic cover, it illuminated a block of black photo frames – all filled with the smiling faces of the company's executives and directors. Mr. Owen could not help but move his eyes across the pictures, looking at the plaques for a name he did not want to see. He found it beneath a frame in the central cluster – beneath a chiselled jaw with ice-white teeth. *Mr. Conran – Managing Director.* She was in the neighbouring frame, wearing the necklace.

Outside the office block, the deathless night waited.

The Gardener

 was busy in the garden when the phone rang, yet again. These days, it's non-stop. I'm beginning to despise that bloody thing. It's worse than having nosy neighbours, I can tell you. How on earth did they get my number, I'll never know. Bloody reporters wanting to know everything!

Storming into the house, I snatched up the detestable object, ready to give them a piece of my mind when the voice on the other end carried me back to when I was sixteen going on seventeen.

'Hello... Is that Jennifer Underwood? It's me... Molly... Molly Maclaren,' the nervous voice spluttered.

In my mind's eye, I'm catapulted back to that dreadful, bone-chilling day. I can clearly see the slate-grey sky and feel the cutting, whistling wind. Remembering the mud-filled cemetery with the two black holes, where they laid my parents to rest.

It makes me shiver even now.

Standing alone, I watched the gravediggers shovel piles of mud as swiftly as they could before the threatening rain began to fall once again. I listened to the hollow sounds that the stones made as they rattled against the coffin lids. Then the heavens opened to receive the souls of the dearly departed while it pisses down on the rest of us.

The Gardener

I shivered. Not because of the icy rain that chilled my face, hands and legs, but a strange sense of foreboding, as I suddenly became aware that I may've been a little too hasty in what I had done.

'I'm sorry to bother you, but it is Jenny, Jenny Sanders isn't it?' the voice drags me back into the present.

'Yes, hello Molly, it's been such a long time. How are you?' I said softly, hearing the child that I never was in the tone of my voice. A persona I've carried with me since discovering that plants, like me, have a darker side too.

My parents were a great deal older than most of my classmates' parents. As a child, you don't see your differences until someone else points them out to you, which my contemporaries were quick to do. No amount of arguing with them could persuade them that they were wrong in their spiteful remarks. The old man, who came to the school gates, was my father.

I can still hear their cutting name-calling, 'Mousy Jenny, mousy Jenny! Grey hair, grey eyes, old and grey before your time... ha, ha, ha! Too grey for your parents, they dumped you on your grandparents... ha, ha, ha!'

So, I gave up, but not before I gave them a taste of my special medicine. At the school Christmas party, I added a few drops to the fruit punch bowl, just enough to make them green, and vomit over their pretty, party frocks.

Once I accepted I was different it was easier. I enjoyed being a bit of a loner far more than trying to conform. To me, my father was far more fascinating than their stupid fathers were, as mine was a botanist.

Plants were my parents' life. What my father didn't know about them wasn't worth knowing. As a child, I spent many a long hour listening to him as he imparted his knowledge to me. He taught me more than just the common or the Latin names for every plant in our garden. Telling me which were medicinal, and which ones are harmful.

'A garden isn't a natural habitat for plants, my little Princess,' he used to say, 'It is man-made. This means every plant in an English garden has come from somewhere else.'

This simple fact sparked a fascination in me to find out more. I didn't just want to know how to grow them, but their history too. Men have fought and died over plants. During the 1500's, a single bulb of a humble tulip became the cause of a war as men's passion raged trying to obtain one of these valuable plants. Throughout the Victorian era, the British became great plant hunters as they built up their collection changing our landscape forever.

Plants are so much more than most people realise. To some the unassuming plants like a Buttercup, Ox-eye daisy, or Rosebay Willowherb is just a weed when they look at them. However, to some a weed can be a thing of beauty, but most won't know how powerful these plants can be. While many enjoy them for their pure aesthetic beauty, a vase of flowers on a sideboard, or even for their healing properties, the thing that captivates me most about plants is their darker side.

I would like to be able tell you that what happened to my parents was an unfortunate accident of fate, but all I can say is lucky for me it turned out to look like one. Being an only child may have many advantages especially when one is young. Not having to share your parents' love and attention may seem wonderful at the time, but as their health declines you find you have to pay it back tenfold, on your own, especially if your parents happen to be elderly. Then that is sooner rather than later.

Like my father, I wanted to be a botanist and travel the world studying plants, but I had to forego my plans when my mother became ill.

Well, not ill as such, but a nuisance.

Although she had a deep love for gardening, it wasn't as strong as my father's was. Now her health was failing, she wanted so much more from life. To do some of the things she'd dreamt about before having to give it all up to support her husband in his chosen career.

The more she complained, the more my father hid out of her reach in the potting shed, leaving me to see to her needs. Since a small child, my mother had always told me I had an old head on young shoulders and that I was more than capable of looking after her and dad as well as myself too.

It started with them being sick. Throughout the day, they became worse, even though I gave them plenty of fluid and some weak, watery soup I made after following a recipe I found in my father's notebook. Fortunately for me, all the plants I needed grew in our garden.

'What on earth is that strange smell, Jenny?' Molly said, coming into the kitchen via the back door without even knocking.

'Goodness me, Molly you made me jump. Couldn't you have knocked?'

'Your Mum never said I had to.'

Molly, a good fifteen years younger than my mother, was her oldest friend. She was constantly popping in to see how I was coping with both my parents' sickness. When I was small she used to look after me whenever they went away for a long weekend when my father used to give lectures on 'The Healing Properties of Plants'.

I never saw her as a replacement mother though I knew she saw me as the child she never had.

'Whatever it is, it doesn't smell right?' she said, opening a window.

'Oh, it's one of my father's medicinal recipes,' I said, with a smile.

'Well, I would've thought the smell alone could kill them. It's awful,' she said, rubbing at her nose with the side of her finger. 'How are they doing anyway?'

'Fine, I think, though I am a little worried. Could you check on them and tell me what you think,' I said, emptying the last of the soup down the sink and adding some bleach to get rid of the smell.

'Okay,' she said heading for the door to the stairs.

Moments later, she had returned, her face pale.

'Call the doctor, Jenny! I don't like the look of them. Something isn't right.'

Molly stayed with me as we waited for the doctor, who came as quickly as he could. When he arrived he told me there was a lot of it about, but because of their age, he wanted to be on the safe side, so admitted them to hospital straightaway.

Within a week of falling ill, my dear parents passed away within a couple of days of each other. At their inquest, the hospital consultant, a kind and gentle man, explained, because of the flu bug, which weakened their immune system, plus their age they were unable to fight off the infection. This, together with the toxins in the contaminated food we'd consumed the night before they fell ill had brought about their premature death. If they had survived, I would've had to spend the rest of my life nursing them.

He said I was lucky not to have gone the same way as them, but being so young had helped me to survive.

The loss of one's parents at such a young age is shocking, I know, but the worst part of it all was the loss of my garden and home too, devastating beyond words really.

It was only after my parents' obituary appeared in our local paper that I found out the truth about our house. An unexpected visit by the owner was the first I knew that we didn't own it, so why hadn't my parents told me that it wasn't ours?

All my careful planning and planting of my garden had gone to waste. It wasn't as though I could just dig it up and move it to somewhere else overnight. I cannot begin to say how angry I felt.

The house had belonged to a friend of my father's, Arthur Kingsmore. His son, Bert explained that the lease on the property ended with the death of my parents and had become his after his father had passed away last year.

'You have two weeks after your parents' funeral to leave my house, unless you can find the money to buy it,' he said with a grin.

Knowing I didn't have the sort of money he was looking for I began to sob. Through my eyelashes, I saw that no amount of crying would melt his heart. My tears were that of frustration more than anything else. Suddenly it began to dawn on me the fruitlessness of what I had done.

As I watched the dreadful little man climb into his car, I picked up my phone and put in an anonymous call to our local newspaper.

'News Desk,' a cheerful voice came on the phone, 'How can I help you?'

'Hello, I'd rather not say who I am, but I have a story, which maybe of interest to your readers,' I said, staring out at my wonderful collection of plants, hoping I could buy myself more time to save my garden.

After putting the phone down, tears began to roll down my cheeks. I inhaled deeply. Wiping them away, I told myself, 'Just get digging. This isn't the time to feel sorry for what you've done.'

On the morning of my parents' funeral as I bent to gather up more pathetic sympathy cards, I caught sight of the headline emblazoned on the front page of the newspaper; ***Tragedy**: young girl made orphan loses family home too.*

I carried the paper through to the kitchen. After dumping the unopened cards onto the work surface with the rest, I began to read the article.

Bert Kingsmore told the reporter that his solicitor was busy drawing up a contract to allow Miss Sanders more time to find alternative accommodation, so he couldn't comment further on the misunderstanding.

Grinning smugly to myself, I switched on the kettle as a wave of satisfaction washed over me.

During the tedious service arranged by Molly, I sat with my head bent trying to look meek rather than how I felt – bored. From all around, I could hear the gentle mutterings from the other mourners. Their concerns and worries drifted over to me as I felt Molly's fat hand patting my arm in a motherly, comforting way.

How I wished with all my heart that it were over, so everyone would just go away and leave me alone.

As my parents' coffins slipped slowly into the cold, wet ground a bitter wind whistled around us. Staring up at the bleak slate-grey sky overhead, my thoughts weren't for my parents, but where was I going to live, and how could I rescue all my most important plants.

'I read about your plight in the paper this morning, Jenny,' a voice said behind me. Turning to see who had spoken, I saw the other mourners dashing for their cars as the rain cascaded down on us.

The voice belonged to one of my neighbours, who now held an umbrella over me as the rain ran in rivulets down my face, chilling my cheeks and soaking through my black jacket and skirt.

'Why thank you kindly, Mr Hampden,' I said smiling up at a tall, rather good-looking widower who lived on our corner.

'Are you here in your car?' he said, as brightly as one could at a funeral.

As I lowered my head to hide my pleasure, an idea began to form.

'Mr and Mrs Maclaren brought me in their car,' I said, trying to muster up some tears. I dabbed at my eyes and thanked the rain.

'Then, my dear, as I will be attending your parents' wake, we shall travel back in mine.'

After he'd closed the passenger door for me, I watched through the windscreen as he dashed, umbrella held aloft, across to Molly who was just getting into her husband's car, and spoke to her briefly. She turned, smiled, and waved to me.

At last, the day from hell, as far as I was concerned was at an end, as Molly helped me to clear away the last of the plates along with a few straggling mourners. After I'd finally convinced them all that I was perfectly capable of looking after myself.

Now all I wanted to do was just get on with potting up my plants into plastic containers. With my seventeenth birthday looming soon, I really didn't feel up to celebrating, though I did hope for some good news from my solicitor, Mister Jarrold sometime during the next week.

Mister Jarrold's call came on my birthday while I was busy in the garden. Dashing to the greenhouse, I quickly shed my dirty gardening gloves and snatched up the phone from where I had left it. Trying not to allow my voice to give away my enthusiasm, I listened carefully as he waffled on about his costs, and that of the funeral, and then he dropped a bombshell. The costs of the repairs needed on the house, through my parents' neglect.

I felt my fervour waning as he explained about a clause in the original lease on the property, that stated my parents were responsible for the maintenance on the house.

My parents' love for their garden was far greater than their love for me, I realised, knowing how much of their time and money they had lavished on it. With no thought for the upkeep of the house that was now going to cost me dearly. In some small way, maybe my mother had been right to complain as she did about my father ignoring what was important and burying his head in the compost heap.

Forking out such a large sum now, meant I would have to forego a place with a garden, as what was left of my inheritance would just about cover the cost of renting a room.

'My dear child,' Mister Jarrold said, 'With such a small amount of money left my advice to you would be to get a job.'

After a polite goodbye, I slammed the wretched phone down in frustration. A job! Any job would do, just something to bring in the money, he'd informed me, taking more of my money no doubt for that piece of advice.

Up as early as I could be, I skipped breakfast and set to work potting up my most valuable plants. Without stopping for lunch, I worked into the afternoon. Suddenly aware of someone standing behind me, I turned quickly, trowel in hand, and found Mister Hampden standing there.

'I'm so sorry to startle you. I did call, but you were so lost in what you were doing,' he said.

I smiled, lowering my trowel.

'I'm so glad you weren't planning to use it on me,' he beamed. 'Have you found somewhere to live yet?'

As I brushed my dark, brown hair back from my grey eyes, I felt the thumb of my muddy glove catch my cheek. In my effort to clean it, I wasn't sure whether I was making it worse.

'Here let me,' he said taking a handkerchief from his pocket and wiped my cheek.

'Please come in. I'll put the kettle on,' I said stepping back from him. I wasn't sure at first what he was planning to say to me, but I didn't want to look too keen. In the warm kitchen as the kettle boiled Mister Hampden sat looking around at the dusty, dirt splattered kitchen units, which Molly had cleaned before the wake.

'Sorry about the mess,' I said coyly, 'I just don't want to

leave any of my plants behind.' I lowered my head and added tearfully, 'They're all I have left of my parents as I must sell everything off to cover my costs, not that I could take much with me. I was so shocked to find out that house wasn't theirs, and to lose the garden too.'

I felt his strong arms around me.

'My poor child, dear girl,' he whispered into my hair. 'I hope you don't mind me saying...' he paused.

I leant into his chest, hoping it would spur him on. He coughed and stepped back from me. Embarrassed, I turned away, adding coffee to the cups and sugar to mine before turning back to him.

'Do you take sugar?' I asked meekly wiping my eyes with the side of my hand.

He drew in a deep breath, 'Jenny, I know I'm a great deal older than you,' he said in a flurry. 'You can say no, if you are shocked by what I'm about to say, but I've spoken to Molly and some of your parents' other friends.'

I narrowed my eyes, and turned back to the coffee making, adding the boiling water while trying to calm myself. 'About what?' I whispered.

'Come to live with me, Jenny. I've that large house and garden all to myself. It would be ideal. You, of course, would have your own suite of rooms. You don't even have to cook for me; I'm quite capable of looking after myself. Even if it's for a short while until you can find somewhere more suitable.' He paused as I turned to face him.

'One sugar or two, Mister Hampden?' I asked smiling.

'Please do call me Henry. One sugar for me, please. So what do you think?'

With my plants settled into their containers, dotted around Henry's large garden, in places I knew were most agreeable for them, I adjusted to my new life. I sold everything belonging to my parents only keeping my personal belongings, a few photographs, my father's old desk, his invaluable notebooks and an array of old gardening books I had collected since a child.

With no worries about household bills, rent, or even food, I knew I should've felt contented. Henry had even provided me with a small allowance, so even my meagre savings was happily growing along with my plants, but still I had a nagging feeling that he was expecting so much more from me.

A year after I had moved in, my suspicions proved correct when one evening after dinner Henry asked me to marry him. At forty-two, he was strikingly good-looking, with a thick head of red hair and a trim body, which he kept fit by running every day. Deciding it would give me some sort of security, I agreed.

After a very showy wedding with all the neighbours in attendance, things settled down and I was able to get back to what was important to me. Early one morning, the following year, as the sun broke through the gap in the curtain, I rose quickly, dressed, and headed for the greenhouse, eager to get started on sowing seeds.

I was happily enjoying the peacefulness of a warm, sunny morning and the feel of the compost in my hands, while busy potting on some Passion Flower seedlings, when my solitude was shattered.

'There you are, Jenny,' Henry said suddenly appeared in the doorway, stepping in, and crowding my space.

I smiled though I felt a nagging feeling slither up from the pit of my stomach. I held my breath knowing he was about ask me something I wasn't going to like.

'You were up early this morning, my dear.' He slipped his arm around my waist.

'I'm sorry I disturbed you, Henry, but I didn't want to waste such a beautiful morning,' I said, focusing on adding another seedling to a fresh pot.

'What are those?'

'These? Oh, they're Passion Flowers.'

'Hmm," he whispered in my ear, 'Passion flower, oh how I wish you felt as passionately about me as you do about your garden.' Turning me towards him, he took the pot from my hand and set it down, where it instantly toppled over.

I went to reach for it, but he stopped me and pulled me in closer.

'Jenny, I've been very patient with you, but now I think its time for us to think about starting a family.'

I looked down at the seedling laying neglected in the warmth of the sun, wanting so much to stop its delicate roots from drying out. Looking up into Henry's blue eyes, I smiled.

'If you make a start on the breakfast, my dear husband, I shall be in soon and we'll talk about it. First, I must finish potting these up.'

He kissed me softly, and whispered, 'We shall do more than just talk, Jenny.' Releasing me, he added, 'Oh, how wonderful it'll be to see little ones enjoying your garden.'

I tried to keep a smile on my tight lips. 'Maybe I can teach them all about growing plants in the same way as my father taught me,' I said as something to say.

'You'll make a terrific mother, Jenny, and teacher too,' Henry said brightly. Then I saw his smile fade as a frown crossed his face, 'Why haven't you planted your collection, and got rid of those horrid plastic containers?'

'Oh, because they don't like having their roots disturbed,' I said through gritted teeth as I turned back to my seedling and tenderly gathered it up.

The funny thing about death is that one is so unprepared for it.

Within a month of our chat about starting a family, Henry became unwell. At night he became so restless that for me to get any sleep at all, he decided to move into the guest bedroom.

Some mornings he was so weak after vomiting through the night, he couldn't get out of bed for work, let alone to run.

On entering his bedroom, he turned his face slowly towards me. Gone were his handsome features. A pale, startled face stared up at me from the white linen sheet. Black smudges under each bloodshot eye seemed to emphasise the hollowness of his cheeks, his full lips now shrunken to thin black lines as he tried to smile at me. On seeing the bowl I had brought, he tried to shake his head.

'Jenny.' His voice seemed to come from afar. 'Your father's concoction isn't helping me; I need a doctor, please.'

'Hush now, you know what they say the worse it tastes the better it is for you,' I smiled. 'But, if you are no better by the end of today, I'll call the doctor. Now drink up,' I said, holding the spoon to his parched lips.

'Promise me, tomorrow, please...' he said, closing his eyes.

'This all started because you wanted a family, Henry, maybe we're trying too hard in the bedroom,' I laughed, wiping his mouth.

He tried to laugh. It came out as a croak. Pulling himself up, his eyes widened as he began to cough violently, shaking his thin frame. Gagging, he vomited evil smelling greenish-brown bile into a bowl, before throwing himself back onto his pillow.

'Please... a doctor, Jenny.'

After many trips to the hospital for tests they couldn't find out what was wrong with him. On his last trip, they decided to keep him in for further tests. This worried me.

After a few weeks, they allowed me to bring him home as his health had begun to improve. Henry was excited, pleased to be coming home, at last, but sadly, six months later, he slipped peacefully away.

At his funeral, Molly sat holding my hand again, but this time I kept the church service short.

'I just can't understand it,' she said at the wake 'He was always such a healthy man, all that running and healthy eating, well, it just goes to show, it isn't good for you. My Harold even said when Henry married you; maybe he should've taken up running if it meant he could catch a pretty, young thing like you.'

I stared at her hard, lowered my head and started to sob. Rubbing at my eyes, I whispered, 'Oh Henry, what am I to do without you...'

'Oh, I'm so sorry. Me and my big mouth. You poor child, all alone again.'

Sweet Henry left me far better off than my parents did, but still I had to move on. I grew to despise my interfering neighbours. Of course, they all hoped that Henry had seeded his little garden.

Forewarned is forearmed as they say. I'd overheard Molly chatting with Harold on my wedding day that maybe Henry would now be lucky enough to have the family he wanted, which he hadn't had with his first wife. Taking no chances, I'd made sure there wouldn't be any patter of tiny feet.

As the gossip became unbearable, I decided I needed to escape and put the house up for sale. Lucky for me, I had learnt my lesson and although a container garden wasn't ideal, it was far easier to move.

At twenty-two, I found out that money doesn't last forever. Well, it seemed such a waste of my life, having to work when I could enjoy having someone to look after me. Deciding it might be fun to do a little travelling, I opted to visit some of the countries my favourite plants came from before settling down to work on a garden of my own. I answered an ad online for a gardening companion and moved into an annex of a house where another avid gardener lived.

Jill, a lovely middle-age petite woman loved gardening almost as much as I did. Intrigued by my mobile garden, she agreed to look after my plants while I did a spot of travelling in exchange for me looking after her house and garden while she went away visiting family and friends around the world.

I know I should've invested my money in buying myself a house with a garden instead of renting, but if I hadn't taken the opportunity to travel when I did, I would never had met James Welland.

Meeting him on the plane may seem romantic, but I'd spotted him earlier while waiting in the boarding lounge. Not quite as good-looking as Henry, he was tall, dark, and mysteriously handsome, but something other than that had attracted my attention. He had a presence about him that made me want to know more.

Before the plane landed at our destination, we were chatting like old friends and I had the information I needed. Single, wealthy with no children, owned a large house and enjoyed having a huge garden, but didn't like gardening though he loved flowers.

What more could I ask for, it doesn't do to have one's partner too interested in one's passion, but just enough not to become bored.

Soon after we met, James asked me to marry him. Of course I said yes. We kept it a simple affair, with just my proprietor, Mrs Price, and James' housekeeper, Mary, and her husband Roger, his driver as our witnesses.

Arriving at my new home, I fell in love with the garden. It was more than I could have dreamt of, with its sweeping lawns, wisteria walkways, ponds, and waterfalls. Through large French windows at the back of the house, I eagerly followed paths that took me to hidden places. Behind red brick walls, and hedges in secret, little gardens, I never knew what I would find until I opened an ornate gate into a gardener's paradise.

When my travelling garden arrived, James insisted that I covered the plastic pots with wonderful pottery containers, if I wasn't going to plant them. Don't get me wrong, I was more than happy, but just a little too apprehensive to let my garden take root.

The thing I loved best of all in James' garden was the large heated greenhouse. In the evenings, while my new husband studied his *Financial Times*, I enjoyed surfing the internet to find more exotic plants I could now grow. Using my father's notebooks, I knew exactly which ones I was looking for.

One evening, I found James watching me over the top of his newspaper. He gave me such a sweet smile. 'Have you for found what you're looking for?' he asked.

'I think so,' I grinned back, 'I can't wait to see if I can grow them.'

'I'm such a lucky man. Most women wouldn't get that excited unless you were buying diamonds and pearls for them.'

I laughed. 'Those things don't grow so don't interest me.'

'You, my darling are the most unassuming woman I have ever met. Lucky for me I had the good sense to marry you,' he said, lifting his paper again.

'Thank you for choosing me,' I said, clicking the pay button for my next order of seeds.

After four wonderful years of travelling and adding to my collection, James asked the dreaded question. Lying in bed one morning, he slipped his arm around my neck and kissed the top of my head. Running his hand across my flat stomach, he whispered, 'My darling, you've made me so happy. Life has been a joy since you became my wife. My dearest darling, I know how much you love growing plants so why don't we grow a family of our own and then my life will be complete.'

I felt my heart sinking as a picture formed in my mind. Rows of my special seedlings wilting in the greenhouse, dying through lack of care and attention while my beautiful garden is becoming a playground for trampling feet, footballs and most awful of all a toilet for dogs and cats. Wherever there are kids there are pets too.

I smiled up at him, 'Of course, my darling, you are right,

how selfish of me not to want to share our happiness.'

That's the thing about life, it can be such a bitch, when you least expect it. I didn't see much point in trying to explain that I didn't want to share my life or garden with kids or pets. If James couldn't see that I was happier on my own, in the greenhouse, with my plants, then he would never understand why I didn't want children.

This time, I took it slowly, allowing my seedlings time to establish themselves, knowing I would need them again soon.

Arriving back from our holiday in Mexico, James' health had deteriorated. As soon as we touched down, he told his driver, Roger when he met us at the airport to take him straight to his doctor.

'You take a taxi home, my darling,' James said to me as beads of sweat gathered on his brow, 'I'm sure it isn't anything serious.'

That evening as I helped him into bed, he told me, his doctor was baffled by his illness and had taken a blood sample before giving him a course of antibiotics believing he may have picked up a bug or been bitten by some insect while we were on holiday.

The next morning after spending most of the night in the bathroom, I suggested he might find my father's herbal soup far more helpful than his doctor's pills. The following night he slept well and in the morning he told me he felt much better.

'Your father's concoction should be bottled up and sold, I feel wonderful this morning, Jenny,' he said as he kissed me.

Leaving James sitting on the patio in the sunshine while we waited for our breakfast, I headed for the greenhouse to check all was well. James had had an irrigation system installed so I wouldn't panic about my plants while we were away. I just didn't trust the young lad, Adam, James had hired to help me in the garden to look after my delicate seedlings. I was just checking my cold frames to see if any of my seeds had germinated, when I heard a heart-chilling scream and a crashing sound.

Dashing along the path to the house, I found Mary standing on the patio with her hands covering her mouth, sobbing, while all around her feet lay the broken remains of the breakfast tray.

James's head hung over the side of the lounger, his eyes stared up at us blankly. From the corner of his blue lips, a thin dribble of black bile stained his chin and the collar of his white shirt.

His hands fascinated me the most. They lay on his lap locked together as though in prayer. I made a mental note to myself to write that down at the first opportunity I got.

'Oh, Mrs Welland, he's dead, is he?' Mary sobbed.

'Come on,' I said, guiding her indoors, 'we'd best phone for his doctor, and then I'll find Roger.'

'My dear, are you all right?' she said patting my arm, and staring into my face.

I bit my bottom lip hard as if I was fighting back the tears. 'It's like losing my parents all over again, Mary, but James wouldn't want me to go to pieces now, the shock might...' I broke off mid-sentence. Lowering my head, I rubbed at my eyes as though to wipe away my tears.

I believe you must make the best of what life offers, so when an opportunity presented itself, I took it. Having got away with it once again, I wanted to enjoy reaping the rewards of my labour, though I was reluctant to have to start my garden again.

However, this time, James had willed everything to me believing I was carrying the heir to his fortune.

Looking back now, I can see I had been too hasty in my decision. While making a repeat trip to our local library to hunt out another list of best-selling crime novels for my new husband, I realised the stark reality of what a fool I had become.

Why me? Why not his bloody lazy daughters? For the last two years, it's the same every week.

Oh I'm sorry, I know I've jumped a bit, but there wasn't anything amazing about how I came to be married to Andrew Picbred.

Anyway, as I was saying, my husband, Andrew, believed in supporting his local library. When his little sweethearts come a calling, I'm sent to collect his latest want list. This is too difficult for his daughters to collect for him on their way over to see him, but no, I have to stop whatever I was doing and travel into town to fetch the books. If I had known he was going to be such a pain I would've started my special treatment sooner.

Every time I saw their car parked outside my house, my blood boiled. Sorry, I should explain something here. Sometimes you don't see what's under your nose. Andrew seemed a nice enough chap, chatty, not too pushy, bit of a laugh really. We met online in a plant forum. Then I kept bumping into him at different flower shows I was attending, as if by accident, of course I now know it was all part of his plan.

Soon he was messaging me online asking if I was going to the next event and could he stay at mine overnight then we could travel together. Slowly, it became the odd weekend and then longer. When he asked me to marry him, I thought as he was practically living at mine that we might as well.

On our wedding day, he suddenly informed me that he'd had to sell his property after his latest business venture hadn't quite worked out to clear a large debt.

With hindsight, I suppose I should've realised he'd been stalking me, but it wasn't until he moved in with his collection of prized tea roses, all potted up in containers, I knew I'd been played for a fool.

The straw that broke the camel's back came when one day I was busy in the greenhouse, and Adam came rushing to find me all in a panic.

'Missus... you better come quick... I tried to stop him, but he... wouldn't listen to me,' he stuttered out, his arms in a flap.

'Adam, calm down it's all right, now slowly. What are you talking about?' I said, moving a tray of pots to the cold frame.

'Mister Picbred... he's digging up some of your plants... saying it's just as much his garden now.'

Hurrying along the path, I followed Adam through to a sunny spot near the patio to find Andrew digging up some of my well-established plants.

'What in the hell are you doing?' I screamed.

'Planting myself a rose garden,' he said, discarding one of my prized monkshood plants. 'I've always fancied having one. You've plenty of the garden left for yourself to allow me to have this small part. Anyway, all you're growing here is weeds.'

I bit my tongue and marked his card, then turned my back on him. What can one say about roses other than they're nice to look at. That's when things really started to go wrong between us.

For a while things settled down nicely. He pruned his roses and lavished his attention on them, leaving me to get on with my main interest. Then his daughters started. I think to save face; he hadn't told them the truth about losing his business. So behaving as though he was the one who owned everything, he allowed them to encourage him in his pursuit of his dream to setting up his rose growing business, by planting more for showing and selling.

I knew they never liked me, but Andrew always said they would come round to loving me as much as he did.

It's a shame that I didn't feel the same about him, or his daughters, Tina and Freda. I certainly wanted to free my life from them, but I knew that would be pushing it just a shade too far, so I had to wait for the right moment.

When Andrew suggested that we should hire a cook and a cleaner after Mary and Roger retired, I was pleased, but then he wanted to hire two professional gardeners and sack Adam because he had damaged one of his precious roses.

'That bloody stupid boy doesn't know what the hell he's doing. Why you've kept him on all these years, God only knows.'

'I've never had a problem with him. He does what I want him to do. He has learning problems, I know, but he's a hard worker and loyal too. It's up to me who stays and who goes, not you!'

During the night I heard Andrew in the bathroom being sick. In the evening he'd dined on a spicy chicken, while I had opted for baked salmon and light salad. After that food didn't seem to sit well with him. Every morning, nausea would hit him in the early hours. He was even unable to keep my soup down. Embarrassed by what was happening to him, he had suggested that we hired a nurse too, but I said no I was his wife so I would look after him. Since his illness, his two darling daughters had kept well away, not wanting to catch the sickness bug, so they told me over the phone.

Every day, he got weaker and paler. Soon some sort of paralysis laid claims to most his body, confining him to a wheelchair. On his good days, he would ask if I could take him to see his roses. Complaining that I had neglected them, he would watch me eagle-eyed as he told me how to prune them.

Saying goodbye to Andrew came easy to me, unlike his daughters. Not only were they angry with me for digging up his awful roses, but also because they found out that they hadn't inherited anything apart from a few of their father's personal pieces. They even had the nerve to accuse me of killing their father. I told them, if they had visited him more often they would've seen how ill he'd become.

When I met Charlie I fell in love. Don't get me wrong, I used the word *love* loosely. To start with he was a lot younger than my normal choice in men. After the trouble I had with my last husband's kids, the last thing on my mind was to rush into anything.

At thirty-five, I wasn't getting any younger. Charlie, ten years older than I, a self-made millionaire, with large brown eyes, good looks and no children was an ideal soul mate for me. For the first time in my life I wanted to settle and have a real marriage that went on forever rather than a few years.

Charlie was such fun. Business trip or not, he would take me with him. Having our own jet plane meant we could go anywhere we wanted to, one day in Paris, then over to South America, following day in China.

I was in heaven. When I went with him, I always hired a car or jeep. While he was in a meeting, I would spend the day seeing my wonderful plants growing in their natural surroundings. I enjoyed that far more than shopping for beautiful clothes, fine jewellery, or works of art. I was happy and I thought he was too.

And for once, death was the furthest thing from my mind.

One day when I came in from the garden, I found him in the library studying the books in my gardening section. Turning toward me he smiled, but instead of lightening up his laughing brown eyes, they looked more like narrow, black slits.

'An interesting collection you have here,' he said patting the spines of the books. He crossed the distance between us then wrapped his arms around me, smiling broadly, but his happiness didn't show in his eyes.

I laughed. 'Why thank you. I didn't know you were interested in gardening, Charlie.'

'We can't know everything about each other. Otherwise, there would be no air of mystique, and that would spoil everything,' he said releasing his hold on me. 'Let's go out tonight. Have a meal somewhere special.'

'That will be lovely. It'll make a nice change,' I said as my eyes scanned the collection of books, that I'd seen him looking at.

'I'm going for a shower,' he said closing the door.

After he'd gone, I crossed to the shelf, and tried to work out which book had caught his interest, but I couldn't tell. Silly I know, but I had kept a few little mementos of my dearly departed ones. Just a few odd photographs of my parents, my happy grooms, and notes on which flowers and plants I like best. Like most passionate gardeners, I kept notes on all my plants i.e. how well they grew, if they were true to form, from cuttings or seeds, and how long they took to germinate as well as their side effects.

Not long after the incident in the library, things began to change between us. Suddenly, Charlie took an interest in the garden and wanted to go to the Chelsea Flower show in London with me.

At first I was excited as he became enthusiastic about growing vegetables. We stood side by side in the potting shed planting up our new seedlings together. He enthused about what squashes he wanted to grow for the village fete, something I never wanted to do even though over the years I had received letters about opening my garden, as others in the village did. To me, it was like showing off and the thought of all those people wandering around, put me right off.

Watching Charlie getting excited about winning a rosette for his first attempt at growing the largest marrow in the village was quite satisfying, and soon we were on first name terms with others gardeners locally. I must admit I was enjoying chatting about the plants I liked to grow with others, though I was always careful about quite what I said.

I don't think you can imagine my shock when I woke one morning to find Charlie on his knees in the bathroom vomiting. Somehow, I managed to get him back into bed and called a doctor.

After the doctor had gone, Charlie told me to stop fussing. It was nothing, just a bug going around. Once I knew he was asleep, I went out to the greenhouse to calm my nerves, telling myself that there couldn't possibly be anything seriously wrong with him.

Over the next few months his health went into decline. No

matter how many trips we took to the hospital for tests they just couldn't find anything wrong with him. I panicked. I argued that there must be something, as a healthy man didn't just land up in a wheelchair without there being something seriously wrong.

The following night, Charlie took a turn for the worst and I rushed him into hospital. I wanted to stay with him, but they sent me home. Alone in our big bed, I sobbed my heart out, never before had I loved anyone as much as I loved Charlie, even my plants in the garden were beginning to suffer as I worried about him.

I just finished my breakfast when I heard a car pull into our drive. Peering out of the kitchen window, I watched as two men with a police officer strode purposely to my front door.

Shocked, thinking something had happened to my Charlie; I hesitated before opened the door.

'Jennifer Underwood,' the taller of the two men said.

'Yes,' I said stepping back from the door.

'Mrs Jennifer Underwood nee' Sanders, I believe?'

'Yes. Sorry what is this about? Is my husband all right?'

'Your husband is fine, but we are arresting you for attempted murder,' he said as he led me to their car.

Me murder Charlie. After all the practice I'd had you would've thought I would have done it properly, if I were going too. Of course, it all came out at the trial. Charlie's uncle had been my second husband. I couldn't believe it. How amazing was that? The day in the library was my downfall. He had found the picture of his uncle in my father's notebook. At least he hadn't understood my coded notes.

Apparently there had been whisperings in Charlie's family that his dear old uncle's death wasn't due to natural causes. Not wanting to suffer the same fate, he got in quick and set me up for attempted murder, which he had hoped would not only lead to a reinvestigation into his uncle's death, but also a settlement on my property too.

What a fool he was to think it would all end there.

You see, I was ahead of the game too. I found out that he'd been losing large sums of money through bad investments and gambling.

The judge smiled at me, when the courts threw the case out. In fact, the verdict was attempted suicide, as Charlie's fingerprints covered the poison plant selection of my gardening book. In the end, the police charged Charlie with wasting their time even though he told them about what had happened to his uncle.

We're divorced now, and I even got a nice little settlement too.

Staring at the phone in my hand, I smiled softly, 'Of course, hello my dear Molly. How are you?'

'I'm fine, Jenny. Good to hear your voice after so long.'

'How's your dear husband, Harold?'

'Sadly, he's no longer with me. Passed away a few years ago.'

'Oh dear so sorry to hear that, must be hard for you now you're alone.'

'My niece Jean and her son, Tom, come to see me whenever they can. Such a clever lad, he found your name and number on the net. He's knows how to find anyone he wants, I think its part of his job, but he doesn't like to talk about it... It's beyond me how they do it. Anyway, how are you?'

'Oh, I was wondering how you found me. I'm so sorry, but I cannot chat for long. I was on my way out,' I said, realising that's how the reporters must have found my phone number too.

'Off somewhere nice, I hope,' Molly asked.

'Out for a meal with Samuel Fairfax, he's such a sweet man,' I said without thinking.

'Isn't he the judge who cleared you? I've been following the court case in the papers and on the television too. Should you be seeing him?'

'There's nothing to stop us now,' I snapped. 'Anyway, he's asked for my help with a gardening problem.' I softened my voice as I stared out at my beautiful garden. 'I'm so sorry, Molly, I really must go. Lovely chatting to you after all these years, but his honour doesn't like to be kept waiting. Call again soon.'

I lowered my phone ready to switch it off.

'I wouldn't rush into this one, Jenny, like you did with the others,' she blurted out.

I felt my heart lurch and lifted the phone to my ear. 'What are you talking about, Molly?'

'What I said.'

'If you're talking about a garden, Molly, one must remember the saying; all good things come to those who wait.'

She laughed nervously. 'I meant, where is Judge Fairfax taking you?'

'Oh, to his. I'm helping him sort out his garden. It used to be his wife's pride and joy before she passed away.'

'I see. So he's wealthy too?'

I detected bitterness in her voice. I laughed, trying to keep it natural. 'What on earth are you suggesting, Molly?'

'Jenny, you know what gossip is like.'

I watched the judge's car turn round on my drive before I spoke again. 'I'm so sorry Molly, I have to go. Samuel has just arrived. Are you still living at the same address?'

'Yes. I am. Do come for a visit, Jenny. It would be lovely to see you.'

'Of course, I shall. We can chat about the old times,' I stared out at my garden, my mind searching for just the right flowers. 'I shall choose something extra special from my garden for you. The flowers look lovely this time of the year. Bye for now, Molly, see you soon. And thank you for calling.'

Fifteen Arthur Cresent

 ifteen Arthur Crescent was a bargain. Not to be missed. To be snapped up, said the estate agent. The owners needed a quick sale. It was four floors high, lofty, spacious, old. It had an Aga, two lounges, a garden with well-kept beds, a shady canopy and a healthy lawn. It had a kitchen and a separate dining room, a games room and a cellar. The decor needed updating, but at such a low price it was to be expected. It had far too many bedrooms for us and it was in a nice part of town. The leafy part. Of course, we took it.

I remember the day that we moved in, it didn't take us very long. We had been living in a small flat and our possessions looked so inadequate and funny when we got them inside the house. They looked like they belonged in a doll's house. We put our two-seater sofa in lounge number one at the front of the house and it was completely over-whelmed by the cavernous room. We wanted to use lounge number two at the back of the house, but we didn't want lounge number one to look bare to the outside world. We're usually not like that, but when we were parading into the house we felt very observed. There was much curtain-twitching in the crescent that morning. This was not unusual in itself. We were fairly young newcomers to the area, women with barely any furniture, of interest.

After we unpacked we sat on the kitchen floor with our backs against our new, old kitchen cupboards. It was a hot summer and I put my hand on your knee and I squeezed it saying,

'We can do what we like here. It's perfect for us.'

You smiled and put your hand on the back of my neck like you do. It was very hot and I could feel a sheen of sweat forming under my hand on your knee already. You leant over and gave me a long and sustained kiss, a deliberate and Zen-like offering. I felt light-headed when we parted and all we could do was just smile at each other for a while. After a moment I even shed one of my ridiculous, solitary tears and you laughed and wiped it away.

'Let's make a list,' you said.

'What sort of list?'

'A list of things we need for the house. Furniture and stuff. What room shall we start with first?'

'The loft,' I said. 'Lets start from the top and work our way down.'

We sat there for the rest of the afternoon and a good part of the evening making lists and talking about our plans for each room, right down to the colours we wanted on the walls and whether we wanted carpets or floorboards. We ate our first dinner in the house on that floor, a bowl of peanuts and a bottle of wine, and we made love there also when the wine was finished. When we went to bed that night you fell asleep first. You were wrapped around me and I listened to our elderly home creak and relax around us both in the cool of night. I remember thinking as I drifted off to sleep, I wish it were tomorrow already.

We had agreed on a space where I could be experimental and artistic with the walls. Deep down I had wanted to be experimental and brave with the design of the whole house but neither of us trusted in me that much. I've got quite a good eye for colour and that sort of thing but it's the actual implementation of my bold ideas that lets me down. We were doing as much of the work on the house as was possible ourselves. If we didn't then we would never afford to furnish the place. Neither of us was very experienced in terms of wallpaper hanging or cupboard fitting. We were going slow and sticking to simple, clean lines and colours, as advised by a television programme on doing up your house and a *Guardian* Sunday supplement.

The *Guardian* supplement had become invaluable to me and I had taken to stuffing it into my back pocket when I wasn't reading it, a bit like builders do with their copies of *The Sun*. You didn't want us to rely too heavily on it because you thought it would be awful to end up with a house that was all somebody else's idea. I largely agreed with you, but it was ever so useful and there were even some stencils that came with it that I was considering using on my artistic wall. Or maybe I would just get some stencils of my own. Thousands of people would have bought the newspaper that contained the supplement so it would be a shame to go to someone else's house and see the same stencilling. Ideally, I would make my own stencils but I'm not very steady with my hands. When I was younger I could never, ever colour in between the lines. It was like some awful pressure, having to try and stay inside those lines. Even when I was managing it, the moment I thought about it my arm would kick out in an involuntary spasm and crash through the borders with crayon. The legacy of this quirk carries through on into my command of scissors and craft knives. Getting me to cut a straight, deliberate or consistent shape with either implement is impossible. I would definitely have to buy my stencils if I wanted them.

I had the stairwell that lead up to the loft. This doesn't sound like much and it's not really, but if it all went wrong then it wasn't going to be too much of a disaster. If it went well and my Michelangelo gene emerged, then it would be a very quirky and lovely detail on the way up to the loft, eye-catching.

I came up to the stairwell at regular intervals in between decorating the rest of the house. I would test colours on the walls from those small tubs that you can buy. It was constantly on my mind. When you were sanding the floorboards in one room and I was varnishing them in another I would be thinking about whether I should paint or paper the stairwell, and whether there should be a border.

A few weeks in and the house was really shaping up. When visitors came around they said things like, 'Ooh! Well!' and they would open their eyes really wide, brows all high and shocked in a pleased sort of way. People were impressed. It was all thanks to the clean, simple lines and colours. A fool could do it but it was very effective. One or two people, the ones who really aren't friends but who had popped around just to be nosy, to see what a house on Arthur Crescent looked like from the inside, looked the most shocked and struggled to paint over their underlying jealousy with smiles. I liked it when those types popped around.

'Would you like a cup of tea?' I'd ask.

'Yes please,' they'd say.

'I'll just pop the kettle on the Aga then,' I'd say. I loved saying that.

I had painted over the wood panelling on the way up to the loft because it wasn't a very fashionable wood and you couldn't really paper over it. Even though it wasn't a fashionable wood, I don't know what sort but it was very light in colour, it would have been a shame not to have taken advantage of its lovely, knotty texture. So that is what I did as I coated it thinly in a bright and snappy yellowy green. It was certainly daring. I had also decided on my choice of stencil. It was a fluid looking shape that was a bit like a wave but not so defined. I wanted it to crawl up the stairwell mirroring the handrail on the opposite wall. It was going to be a sharp lime colour.

I had done everything I wanted in the stairwell by now except for the stencilling. It was late in the afternoon and the natural light was melting away. I would leave the stencilling to another day. I wanted to get it perfect and I needed the light for that. I placed the stencils, the lime green paint and the sponge with which I would apply it on the bottom step of the well.

I went up the stairs to have a look around the loft. Although we had explored it when we first moved in, we hadn't been up much since. It was the first room we had talked about decorating but we decided that it should be the last we would actually tackle. It was a huge space, like a ballet studio or a hayloft. We were considering making it into a guest suite with a shower and a bathroom but that depended on our funds. At first I thought it would be perfect as my study. I liked the idea of being perched up high away from things. The problem was that it was so hot. Far too hot when the sun hung directly above the skylights late morning. It generated a heat that lingered all day and intensified throughout the afternoon. It was so hot that I suspect you could have grown tomatoes up there.

As well as the skylights there were a number of other windows that looked down onto our small gravel drive. I heard your car pulling into it and I walked over to the window to watch you arrive home from work. You had turned off the engine but you weren't getting out. You would have been collecting your stuff together. Perhaps you were listening to a voicemail or reading a text? It was quiet in the loft and I stood there wilting, waiting to see you appear from the car. I could have gone downstairs to meet you when you came in but I just stayed there, in silence. What were you doing? You were certainly taking your time. I concentrated on breathing in and out. It must have been minutes and there was no sign of you. I couldn't see into the car from my position so I still had no idea what you were doing. By now I decided that you must have been taking a long phone call from a friend. I pushed the window open, placed an arm either side of its frame and stuck my head out to get some air. It was better than a cold glass of mineral water. It was clean and fresh and I laughed out loud. I thought it was so strange that from my neck down I felt as though I was trudging through a desert, yet my head was enjoying an atmosphere that was as crisp and clear as a mountaintop.

You placed your hand on my shoulder, I screamed and jumped, hitting my head on the top of the window frame. I turned around and saw it was you. By now you held me from the waist.

'What are you doing?' I yelled.

'Shhh. Shhh. Are you okay?'

'I could have fallen out the bloody window! What were you doing?'

'I've been calling you for ages.'

'But you haven't even left your car.'

You looked at me quizzically. You took your right hand from my waist and placed it over my hand on my head where I was instinctively rubbing at the rapidly swelling lump.

'You've had a nasty knock. You should lie down.'

'I don't want to lie down. What happened?'

'You hit your head.'

'Yes, I know I hit my head. Why were you creeping about?'

'I wasn't creeping about. When I came up here and found you, you were quite far away. What were you doing?'

'I wasn't doing anything. I was waiting for you.'

Then I told you about hearing the car on the gravel and the fact that I hadn't seen you get out. You said that it was strange but that perhaps I should lie down anyway. Later, after dinner when we were curled up on the new three-seater sofa, you suggested that maybe I had just gone to the window too late and that you had probably already left the car by the time I was peering at it. That was the most logical explanation. It didn't feel like it though, not to me.

That weekend we pottered about the house seeing to details. I went to the supermarket and bought all the ingredients for something I could cook slowly. Something that would fill the whole house with a smell like a real home, a stew. When I came back and set to work on the stew you came in through the back door to tell me what you had found in the shed. An ancient lawn roller, some rusty old tools and a selection of terracotta plant pots. We discussed what we should keep and what we should get rid of. We weren't convinced that we'd use the lawn roller, but it was too bulky take down to the tip. Perhaps we could Freecycle it and someone would come and take it off our hands? Did anyone use lawn rollers any more?

I put the stew on a low heat set to cook for the rest of the day. You went back down to the shed and I decided that I would finally complete my stairwell with the stencilling. When I got to the stairwell I saw that the stencilling had been started. The first segment had been painted on and the stencil was smudged with the lime green paint. I wondered why you had decided to begin it, especially when we had agreed that it was my project. I was annoyed and even thought about how I could justify completely losing my temper. I checked to see if the stencilling was begun in the place I had wanted it. It was, so I couldn't even storm down to the shed and declare that you had done it incorrectly. It was a rather neat start and I carried on where you had left off.

It didn't take too long to get the job done and in just over an hour or so it was complete. I noticed that my stencilling wasn't quite as neat as your initial effort. Luckily, to the unknowing observer it wouldn't actually be that obvious. It bothered me though because I could see it. I would always know it was there and I was a little angry that you were bound to see that my attempts weren't as professional as yours. You would never say so being far too considerate, but you would know. I thought this really unfair, when all I had wanted to do was to save the decoration of the stairwell for myself.

I went downstairs and found you. You were kneeling over the toolbox in the utility room, filing away some of the salvaged tools from the shed. I told you I had finished the stairwell and you looked up towards me with a proud and excited grin. You stood up, brushed your hands against the back of your jeans and said,

'Well, lead the way.'

You followed me up through the house chatting about how brilliant you were sure it would look. I felt a little guilty, like I was leading a condemned woman to the gallows. I wouldn't be able to hold it in, my annoyance, even though I knew it would be the more loving thing to do. I knew it didn't matter really. It was your house too and it was only a daft stencil. But, there you were, all excited and supportive and there I was, fuming.

'Wow! It's beautiful,' you said when you saw it. You thought the colours really worked and that we should have let me go wild with the rest of the house. You gave me a kiss on the cheek and then sat on a step to look around and admire the green and yellow view.

'How come you started on the stencilling?' I asked.

You said that you hadn't and you furrowed your brow looking to me for an explanation. I explained and did well to hide my annoyance. I made myself sound more bemused about the situation.

'You must have started it yourself darling. Perhaps you forgot?'

As if I would forget. That was a ridiculous comment to make and I told you so. The last time I'd been anywhere near the loft was when I had banged my head. You said that was the last time you'd been there too. It wasn't exactly an argument but we were clearly both irritated and the atmosphere in the confined space was uncomfortable.

'I don't know what you want me to say.'

I didn't either. We dispersed into the afternoon and didn't bring the topic up again.

Your invisible and silent entrance into the house and the mysterious stencilling incident weren't the only two things to happen there to make me look like I was losing the plot. There were other things such as the strange case of the disappearing, extendable ladder (found in the loft), the mysterious relocation of an entire underwear drawer (found in the loft) and the curious laughter that occasionally echoed throughout the house (emanating from the loft). This you found particularly curious as you said it sounded like my laughter.

It was the laughter that really brought it home to you, purely because we heard it a number of times when we were both in the second lounge. You knew that it could not have been me making the noise. The final incident, the one that made us decide to put the house on the market was the first to relate directly to you. It was a few days after the laughter had died down. You were walking up the driveway having been to the shops for milk and the paper when you looked up to our bedroom window and saw me staring out of it. You said that I looked all dreamy and far away like when I had my head stuck out of the window in the loft. You waved at me and caught my attention. I looked you straight in the eye then moved behind the curtain that was next to me. Wondering what you had done to deserve such a strange response you entered the house calling my name. I shouted that I was in the bathroom and you came to me. I was lying in the bath, relaxing with a book. I had obviously been there for some time. I had certainly been there for about fifteen minutes, in fact I'd read at least ten pages since you had left for the shops. You were alabaster white when you realised. You knelt down and gripped the edge of the bath.

'Get undressed and join me,' I said.

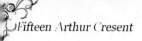

You took off your clothes, climbed in and sat in front of me between my legs. I slid my arms around you and hugged you. I rocked you in a delicate and controlled way. I kissed the back of your neck.

'We'll go, we'll leave this place, we'll go,' I said.

And we did.

The Alphabet's Shadow

ergus had died a few weeks earlier, the lump on his tail growing from a pea to a nut to a ball. Four inches in diameter, yet who could measure the death within? I wept like a baby, my wife like a mother, the vet like a Russian. 'Fergus, Fergus', we cried, 'where goest thou now?' We scattered his ashes by the skip near the playing fields, each telling the other that we'd never go back. Why go? Leaves fell, dogs pissed, yet Fergus would never know. Ho, what could he tell us of the passage of the hours? Branches broke, wood rotted, the jetty fell in to the pond – and all the while Time, that old bastard, hunched nonchalantly by the fire-damaged shelter, slowly winding his watch...

I can't remember how long it was before I went back: two weeks, three weeks more? It was autumn, gusty, clouds unravelling like old wool, but there I was, sitting on our bench, hat damp, trousers green, the ghosts of old biscuits lining my pockets. What was I thinking about? Nothing, I was thinking about nothing. My lips were dry, my nose gummed, my head a bucket from which all thought had drained. And yet, oddly, it was just when I was thinking of nothing that I saw it, scampering in the half light. What's that, what was it? Well, I don't know: both a squirrel and not a squirrel – the remains of a squirrel, perhaps.

'Hello little fella,' I said.

The thing looked flattened, mangy, like a hair piece left out in the rain. Its nose was squashed, its eyes all yellow and yolky.

'Hello,' I said. 'Hello wee man.'

Such a sight, such a thing! But what was it – puppet, road kill, pet? It scampered to and fro amongst the trees, flicking its tail and clicking erratically. Then, just as I started to lose interest it pointed at me with its little black gloves, and gestured for me to come hither. S' true! Half of me – my legs, feet, my aching knees – started to get up, but the other half – head, shoulders and torso – stayed rigid: I was like two people, one awake and one asleep, a toy where the top and bottom don't fit. So you can imagine my surprise when I found myself traipsing off into the darkness, my feet two heavy clods of earth, my legs as stiff as fence posts. What did I think I was doing? Why follow this thing? And yet for all that, the squirrel (squirrel?) led the way and I followed, its tail coming and going in the gloom like a hand up a sleeve.

The rag scuttled across boggy ground and then headed for a dense clump of trees. There were muddy patches, deep furrows, upturned roots: and me with my knees! But when I stopped to point at myself it nodded and flicked its brush impatiently. What could I do? At the edge of the trees it was snapped inside like a rat on a string. I breathed in and took the plunge. The copse was bigger than it looked: black leaves, black torsos, black bark. I mean, would it kill the council to put up some lights? Out of breath I rested my palm against a wet and darksome tree, my fingers stinging as they rubbed against the great black shape. Gingerly, I felt whorls, flourishes, a rigid and ageless sea. But what was this: a key, a pattern, a shape? All of a sudden my fingers started to grip harder, burrowing deep into the soft, rotten heart. What was I doing? I felt my nails clawing, my digits grasping, tearing. When I pulled my hand away, my fingers were as earthworms, all pale and long and jointless. The skin at the end was torn. Something black and painful had splintered inside one nail. 'Oh, what has become of me?' I thought. The squirrel had departed. Nuts rained down from the sky.

When I got home, I locked myself in the bathroom and guiltily scrubbed my nails. The cuticles were green, the tips black, my digits as ten runner beans. The fingers of a gardener or a corpse? A grave-digger, maybe. Anxiously I switched off the light and ate lasagne with my wife.

ii

It was pretty dark by the time I finished work, so I parked up on the waste ground near the playing fields and made straight for the bench, making my way through the mud as furtive as a crow. The park was cold, colourless, silent – even the starlings had stopped complaining. Out in the darkness, the trees held each other up like drunks, their roots as tangled as string.

'Hello?' I said. 'Hello, wee man?'

Ah, no brush, no paw, no little yellow eyes; instead, the gloom went on forever. But why then had it beckoned me here – just to rub my nose in the void? I reached one hand toward the column of trees and then pulled it back: I should listen to a rodent? And yet for all that, I couldn't seem to help myself. The trunk was rutted, gnarled, lined with deep furrows. Was that an arrow? And inscribed next to it – some kind of cross? Anyway, that's when I saw it: sad, wrinkled, stooped over as if looking for its glasses, the ruin of a once great thing. Swiftly I produced my papers and peeled back my crayon, rubbing as hard as I could. The paper crumpled and the crayon slipped, but that didn't stop me – instead I rubbed and rubbed till the whole sheet was filled. But what did the strange frenzied frottage mean? It was too dark to see. In the half-light there were squirrels *everywhere*.

Only in the light of the dashboard did everything start to become clear. The rubbing had produced a rough kind of map, or at least some kind of rough sketch, the dark, scribbled marks held together by long strings of black. Here the shelter and there the poo-bin; next to it the playing field, the vandalised posts inscribed. And yet somehow, I couldn't quite read it. No, really! I turned the chart upside down, twisted it this way and that, screwed up my eyes and squinted, but all to no avail; it was both the park and yet not the park – the park's shadow perhaps. When I looked up an inky shape rolled past my line of vision and disappeared behind the car.

'Man or squirrel?' I yelled. 'Man or squirrel?'

I switched on the headlights but if anything the outside became only darker, shapes and forms turning into one dense block. Disappointed, I slid the paper into the glove compartment and drove the long way home.

iii

'I thought about going back to the park today,' she said, stirring the beans thoughtfully.

'Really?'

'Mm. You know, to his place.'

'Ah…'

'Just to… I don't know.'

For a long moment I held my breath.

'Did you go?'

'Go?'

'Back, I mean.'

'No… I… I just wanted to…to…'

'Shh, come here…'

'It's not that, it's just…'

'Shhh, it's okay…'

I held her and felt a painful black splinter pressing in under my nail. Every time I touched it, I felt pain. The whole finger looked strange.

'Shh,' I said. 'Why cry? No, really. Why?'

iv

Stuck in traffic I furtively slid the sheath of papers out of the glove compartment and spread them out on my lap. Yes, lines, shapes, patterns. But what did they mean? 'Twas a chart without landmarks, a language without a dictionary, a maze with no way in. This a strawberry and that a grave? There a boat and next a breast? Then the lights changed, and these too, were gone.

Just imagine: a world folded, encrypted, a signpost without arms. Over lunch, I photocopied the markings again and again, seeking out arrangements, symbols, pictures. Was that a nose or a fountain? An eye or a hole? If I folded flap A over side B, creased side 1 over page 1.2, would it all start to make sense? O reader! I spent the best part of the day measuring, squinting, moving pieces of paper back and forth across my desk, but alas, 'twas not to be: this was a door I could not budge. I mean, what if the squirrel lied to me - what if there were no anagrams, no hieroglyphics, no key at all? What if I was wrong about everything? Between my eyes, the dots and the page, something refused to meet. A tome without a title, index, letters of any kind: who could keep one's page?

That night, after dinner, I snuck off to the kitchen to unfurl the Dead Sea scrolls, the TV talking to itself in the corner. Tracing the lines and rounding the hills, I started to feel more optimistic: wasn't that the bridal-path and that the latch-gate, that the big hill on the rise above the car-park? But then the typography started to fade and the shapes once more turned to smears, shadows, blurs. Squiggle or road? Mark or tear? I could not tell. These were instructions in another language, signals from a sinking ship. My wife was upstairs crying and I binned the papers in disgust. Where to go, what to do? I cupped my ear to the night, but the night wasn't talking. When I went upstairs, my wife wasn't talking too.

That same night, I was awoken by a powerful need to urinate, an urge which dragged me out of bed, across the hall, and off to the bathroom at the end. Even my piss looked green. 'Diabetes!' I thought, shaking my head in sorrow. Ah, how terrible I felt! My tongue was dry, my skin bad, nails foul.

Bleary-eyed, I padded down to the kitchen, my hand hurting as if someone had driven a needle deep below the nail. Abruptly the back door rattled and the security light came on. Blinking, I wandered over to the window, peering out at the gloom: first a blur, then a shadow, finally a thing, four legged and shaggy, hobbling past the tool shed and shuffling toward the bins. No, really – s'true! The thing moved awkwardly, limping on two good legs, its back-end sloping as if struggling uphill. But what was it - fox, dog, beast? The thing was closer now, half way between nothingness and the house. My eyes throbbed, my fingers ached. I needed to pass water again, and perhaps the other too. The fox (fox?) knocked over the bags by the garage and started to root inside, pulling one of the bags out into the centre of the lawn and lying there, its jaws methodically clacking. Such a thing! The animal was all wet and matted, two yellow eyes leaking onto its snout. It was only when I saw it cough up a ball of paper that I realised why it had come: as a messenger, a sign, a communiqué from the other side!

The moment I went outside the fox (fox?) vanished, its shadow no more than a smudge or smear. Outside, there was stuff everywhere: wrappers, crisp packets, sanitary towels. The wad of paper lay on the grass, like a ball or a poo. Yes, saliva-spattered, punctured by teeth marks, an enormous stain down one side: my map, my chart, my clue! Looking at it again, it was as if somebody had slipped a pair of glasses miraculously upon my eyes. I mean, just look at it! There the park, here the lake, yonder the bog garden to the east. And there, right at the side of the gardeners' hut, a cross, an 'x', the universal sign for 'dig here'.

Breathlessly, I dressed and retrieved our spade from the shed. My wife was sleeping, our neighbours likewise. I was still in my slippers, but why worry? I climbed into my car and drove away, the need to pee coming and going in bursts. Fortunately the park had no gate, no security. It was dark, but there were still a few street lights, bushes, stumps, signs. It was cold but not terribly so; if anything I seemed to be running a fever, sharp pains radiating from my groin and advancing on my chest in waves. First I buttoned my coat, then I checked the chart, and finally I started to dig; the ground was soft and inviting and the digging seemed to take no effort at all. No sooner had the spade entered the ground then a great clod of earth lay by my side. Another step down and a second great clod appeared. Ho, why sweat? I dug and dug and pretty soon the thing was done. My trousers were muddied, my fingers black, my slippers ruined, but what did I care? There they lay on the ground before me: a plastic shopping bag, a twisted spoon, a dog lead, string. Yes, it was starting to make sense now, the next step on the bridge!

It was only after I'd cleared up that I noticed a figure watching me, though whether man or woman, young or old, I couldn't really tell. Why ask, I thought, why worry? Let them watch, take notes, tell! The figure was scribbling in a notebook, his (her?) face obscured by the night's inky thumb. I got home about three. My wife was asleep. I was covered in mud. Greenish darkness covered my arms right up to my elbows. And my slippers? We will not talk of my slippers. After kissing my wife I climbed under the covers and fell into a deep and bottomless sleep.

v

The next morning I put the sheets in the washing machine, poured myself a drink, and went off to find the bag. No point going to the office today: no time! Instead I opened the plastic carrier and arranged the objects in neat little rows, setting out the objects in terms of size and significance. Each of the items obviously referred to a different section of the park: the spoon, the café, closed down years ago, the bag, the Spa, haunt of glue-sniffers and alcoholics, folk buying lighter fluid late at night. And the dog lead? This seemed less certain. Bag dispensers, benches, trees? The string formed a noose and I hid it beneath my desk.

The next step was to spread the items out on the carpet, cushions for hills, a wash bowl the lake, a line of pens for footpaths. Only the dog lead confused me: stopping points, sniffing posts, playing fields? Or what if it were the shape or the texture which was the clue rather than the thing itself? Ho, what if the answer were engrained in the very texture of things? My skin itched, my nails throbbed, my eyes watered. And then it came to me: the waste-ground, the skip, Fergus – tch, what else should it be? Yes, the dots joined to form a circle, a wheel, a hole. But on the other side, what? Another hole?

Well, the park was a good deal busier than I'd imagined. Middle-aged men carried rucksacks and notebooks, scruffy-looking guys sketched the lake, old women wandered about with pens. But what were they looking for, what did they want? Instantly I felt suspicious: why the crafty look in their eyes, wither their feverish steps? Some skinny guy in a hat eyed up my charts. A bearded gentleman holding his schnauzer nodded in my direction. Two school kids, bunking off class, compared notes. All was a puzzle, a cryptogram, a work-sheet…

Pinned to a tree was a sign for a lost dog, the writing spidery, the page half torn. Even the dog seemed just a blur, a shape, an inky smear of fur. Only its yellow eyes looked real.

And at the bottom? Yes, a phone number. Somebody answered on the second ring.

'Hello?'

The line clicked and whirred but I could hear no voice.

'Hello? Um, I'm calling about the dog…'

Nothing. No answer. The winds of time.

'Ah, is there anybody there? Because…'

More clicking.

'Hello?'

There was a shuffling sound and all of a sudden I felt embarrassed. If someone were to answer, what should I say? I didn't have the dog, hadn't seen it, didn't have a clue. What was I doing on the phone at all?

'Ah, well, the dog, it…'

The line clicked again and then went dead.

When I phoned back there was more clicking, perhaps some breathing too.

'Hello?'

The last time the thing had gone to answer-phone.

'Fergus! Fergus! O friend, are you there?'

I don't know; maybe the number wasn't the clue. Maybe it was the handwriting or the paper used, or the shape of the animal's head. Fingers tingling, I settled down on a half-vandalised bench, examining the graffiti, the rust marks, the place where somebody had tried to set fire to the slats. Some hooligan had written 'Dave Hays Wears His Ma's Pants' in permanent marker: heaven knows the reason why.

Across the way some guy in a business suit marked up a preliminary report on the rain shelter, noting cracks, lines, angles. Two waiters argued over their sketch of the council toilets. A woman dressed all in black studied an enormous clip file as if slowly taking in the rules of the game. Yes, all was a game, a scheme, a text. But how many players and to what end?

All I knew was that the contestants were everywhere; the guy in the wheelchair, the birdwatcher with his binoculars, the mathematician and her set-square, all of them noting, drafting, setting down. One studied the lines in the flagstones, another the contours of the hill; one counted the number of rubbish bins, his mate grubbing inside them, examining, measuring, recording. And if all this information were laid end to end? Why, such paper would form a pathway, a passage, a ladder from one place to the next…

Next to such encyclopedic efforts, my own poor investigations seemed awful small. What did I have? The gestures of a squirrel and the ball of a fox. And all the time my fingers angrily throbbed and grew. One nail was loose, another had fallen away entirely; even holding a pen felt increasingly difficult. How then was I supposed to compete? Down by the boating lake some woman ticked off the number of railings in her pad, touching each bar with her glove before staring off into space. For some reason she seemed awfully familiar but for a moment I couldn't place her. And then it occurred to me: my wife! But why wasn't she at work – my scrupulous, conscientious, work-driven wife? I watched her checking and rechecking her numbers, comparing the number of railings with the number of ducks on the island. Was it her? Someone in her coat? Then some joker drifted in front of me and she was gone. Eighteen railings, seven ducks, one moor-hen, but wives: none. Swiftly I pulled out my phone and punched in her number.

'Hello?'

The line clicked, but that was it.

'Hello? Um, I'm calling from the park…'

Nothing. No answer. The winds of time.

'Um, is there anybody there? Because…'

More clicking.

'Hello?'

There was a shuffling sound and all of a sudden I felt embarrassed. If she were to answer, what should I say? I hadn't solved the puzzle, opened the map, found the answer. I mean, what was I doing on the phone at all?

'Um, you see…'

The line clicked again and then went dead.

When I phoned back there was more clicking, perhaps some breathing too.

'Hello?'

Next time the thing had gone to answer-phone.

'Jo? Jo, are you there?'

The trees waved their arms in alarm.

'Jo?'

Come to think of it, the blurred shape on the flyer looked a little like my wife too – the shape of her hair, the angle of her chin, the funny little scar above one eye. But she also looked liked the ring-road around the perimeter, the traffic lights and roundabout, a map of the principality. Upside down one could see roots, trunks, arms, a copse of fist-shaking sycamore. And if one squinted *just right* the very grains of the paper produced inky pools, dark smears, lost tributaries. But which clue was correct? The last four digits were 2355: half a hair to midnight - or some other code or rune? Whatever it was, I shredded the paper before one of my opponents could discover it.

vi

By now it was a little after six but I didn't feel like going back home. What if my wife were there? What if she had figured things out? I wasn't hungry but I forced myself to go and eat a pasty and chips, carefully counting each chip, pushing the peas this way and that on my plate. Seventeen chips, thirty one peas. On one side of my plate, the peas formed a river; on the other, the ketchup formed the shape of an owl. O, reader! It was as if the very edge of reality were peeling back like an envelope. I mean, what if everything – the tables, the chairs, the stains on the waitresses' apron - were a clue? Everything meant something, but anything could also be another thing entirely. Ho, even the tiles on the floor contained sequences, arrangements, paths. On the verge of a great revelation – I had a funny metallic taste in my mouth and my limbs felt oddly brittle – I staggered from my seat and left the joint, running. The world was a newspaper in which I could not read a single word. When I closed my eyes I saw blobs. When I opened them again the blobs formed shapes. But what kind of shapes – and why such tiny print? Fortunately my car wasn't too far away. Locking the door I gripped the wheel hard. My fingers looked like ten black tubers starting to sprout. Even turning the ignition felt hard. And I was supposed to hold a pen with these?

Fortunately as soon as I got away from the city centre and coasted along the long, looping dual-carriageways, my mind started to cool down, my thoughts again becoming my own. Slowly the two halves of my brain started to knit, my lips moving to the music, my numb, greenish fingers drumming along to the beat. How long did I drive for? I don't know. Long enough for the light to slip between the cracks! At 21.19 I stopped at Crossley services. There was a guy filling in a puzzle book, and another finishing a crossword, but as for other players, that was about it. I had a cup of tea. My piss was still a little green. At 22.33 I pulled into a lay-by because my fingers were so awfully sore. How ugly they were! Without print or ring or nail. I felt terribly embarrassed but couldn't seem to be able to find my gloves anywhere. My fingers were terribly long, the tips strangely old and fermented. At 22.56 I headed back into the city, passing the industrial estate, the out of town shopping centre, the DIY store. I drove round and round the same six streets very slowly. The pavements were empty. The traffic was very light. It was as if a series of black shutters were coming down, one after the other. O, this dark! A dead pigeon lay by the side of the road, its broken body pointing crookedly toward the park.

The park? When I got there, there wasn't a parking space *anywhere*. I'm not kidding! Car-parks, pull-ins, side-roads: all jammed. I ended up parking nearly four blocks away, walking along back alleys past shuttered garages, purposefully avoiding the graffiti and the cats.

Even the air felt filled in somehow, big blocks of scribbled black. And yet, despite the number of vehicles – four by fours, people carriers, land rovers, saloons, even a mini bus or two – there didn't seem to be anybody about. The cars were parked half on and half off the pavements, in places two deep, but I couldn't see a single pedestrian, not so much as a single bum. Where was everybody? Street lights formed fuzzy circles, iron railings leaned against each other, the post-box licked its lips. Yes, I thought, this must be the place! I picked up a stick and tapped the ground though in truth there was plenty of light, at least if one kept to the path. Elsewhere thick barrels of nothingness oozed out over the grass, the autumn night gulping shadows. Was I scared? No, not really. Only my hands worried me, my long, green fingers itching from the inside.

Heigh ho! The gates to the park were open, rubbish blowing across from an upturned bin. Take away wrappers, crisp packets, newspapers, plastic bags: so, I thought, more clues! A green mitten was hung on a railing. A puddle formed the letter 's'. Somebody had moved the benches so they formed a kind of circle. Yes, yes, this was it; I followed the path between two great banks of darkness, smelling mulch, piss, November. The darkness was a great mouth but I didn't let it worry me. What I feared was a gravestone marked: He Sought But Did Not Find….

Cracks formed messages on the path. Stones made full stops. A broken umbrella looked like an exclamation mark. And what of the other readers? Had they turned the page? I thought about the parked cars but still couldn't understand it. There were shadows, but not the things which cast shadows. Or had I got it the wrong way round? What if it were the shadows which cast things after all?

At 23.55 the phone rang.

'Nick?' asked my wife. 'Nick, where are you?'

I didn't answer.

'Listen, I've been home. What happened? Are you okay? Nick, what is it?'

The wind blew and the trees shook.

'Nick?'

'Shh,' I said. 'Why cry? No, really, why?'

I lifted one foot from the path and strode out into the void; the lights behind me faded until they were less than the size of a pea. Were there stars? No, there were no stars. No sky, no up, no down. And yet even here my eyes started to adjust, blurs forming bushes, holes, hands…

The dog (dog?) was waiting for me at the edge of the trees, panting softly, its yellow eyes dripping.

'Fergus?' I said. 'Fergus, is that you?'

Its mouth clacked open and shut with a snap.

'Fergus?'

I walked the last part of the way blind, neither caring for mud nor shit nor roots; instead I followed the eyes as I would a lantern, entering into a wood far larger than found on any map.

In here, the trees looked old and tired. Some of them bent down to tie up their roots, while others pointed uncertainly toward the heavens above. How ancient they seemed! When I touched them it was touching the skin of an old dead animal – an elephant, perhaps. The bark contained valleys, inlets, channels; when I pressed down I felt a kind of hinge, a pivot on which the whole of the world seemed to turn. Ah, such a place! Above me the leaves formed letters, lines, words, a whole alphabet silhouetted against the sky. When I looked down, my feet were covered in mud, two great clods planted in the earth. My torso was a great gnarled trunk, my arms crooked black boughs, my fingers twigs ending in vowels and consonants and commas. What had happened to me? What did it mean? Near the top branch a crow watched me with cruel yellow eyes.

'What does it mean?' I yelled. 'Why can't I read?'

The crow pecked at my buds and winked. The wind blew the trees. Letters tumbled all around me.

'Read?' it said.

And with that its wings snapped shut like a book.

Contributor's Notes

Alan Bilton was born in York in 1969 and teaches literature, film, and creative writing at Swansea University. He is the author of two novels (both part slapstick comedy, part surreal anxiety dream) – *The Known and Unknown Sea* (Cillian Press, 2014) and *The Sleepwalkers' Ball* (2009) – as well as books on silent film, contemporary fiction, and the 1920s.

Mark Blayney won the Somerset Maugham Prize for *Two Kinds of Silence*. His story 'The Murder of Dylan Thomas' was a Seren Short Story of the Month and he's published poems and stories in *Agenda*, *Poetry Wales*, *The Interpreter's House*, *The London Magazine* and *the delinquent*. His second book *Conversations with Magic Stones* was described by John Bayley as 'remarkable… as good as some of the best of Elizabeth Bowen's, and praise does not go higher than that.' Mark performs comedy as well as MCing regularly and his new one-man show *Be your own life-coach… with ABBA* tours this year. More info at www.markblayney.weebly.com

Shirley Golden's stories mostly wing their way back to the recesses of her laptop and await further coffee-fuelled sessions of juggling words. Her short fiction has found homes in the pages of magazines and anthologies, or in various corners of the internet; a few have won prizes. She is door-person and arbitrator to two wannabe tigers, and can sometimes be found

on Twitter when she should be writing. Find her at www.
shirleygolden.net or @shirl1001.

Carly Holmes was born on the Channel Island of Jersey and lives
on the west coast of Wales. She has an MA in Creative Writing
from UOW Trinity Saint David and has just completed her PhD
in Creative Writing. A number of her short stories have been
published and placed in competitions. Carly is Secretary for the
PENfro Book Festival committee and organises The Cellar Bards,
a group of writers who meet in Cardigan monthly for a lively
evening of spoken word, and she's also on the editorial board of
The Lampeter Review. When not doing any of the above, Carly can
usually be found in her garden, talking to her hedge sparrows.
Her debut novel *The Scrapbook* was published by Parthian in 2014.

Howard David Ingham has written fiction, poetry, theatre
and games since 2002. He has been published worldwide,
is an accomplished performer, and was artist in residence at
Swansea University from 2012–13. He is currently working on
comic series *Transhuman Resources*, a satire dealing with issues
of capitalism, race and gender, in collaboration with Ashur
Collective, Detroit.

Amanda Mason lives in York and writes plays, flash fiction and
short stories. She's had work published online by *Spontaneity* and
Flash Gumbo, and short stories included in collections produced
by Cracked Eye, *Storms, Lies and Wildcards*, *The Fiction Desk*, *New
Ghost Stories*, and in the National Flash Fiction Day Anthology,
Eating My Words. She is currently working on her first novel.

Jo Mazelis' collection of stories *Diving Girls* (Parthian, 2002) was
short-listed for Commonwealth Best First Book and Welsh Book
of the Year. Her second book, *Circle Games* (Parthian, 2005) was

long-listed for Welsh Book of the Year. Her novel *Significance* was published by Seren in September 2014. She lives in Swansea.

Kate North writes fiction and poetry. Her novel, *Eva Shell*, was published in 2008 and her poetry collection, *Bistro*, in 2012. She lives and teaches in Cardiff. Find her at www.katenorth.co.uk.

Bethany W. Pope is the author of three poetry collections, *A Radiance* (Cultured Llama, 2012), *Crown of Thorns* (Oneiros Books, 2013), and *The Gospel of Flies* (Writing Knights Press, 2014). She has two forthcoming collections, *Undisturbed Circles* (Lapwing), and *Persephone in the Underworld* (Rufus Books). Bethany is an award-winning author of the LBA, and a finalist for the Faulkner-Wisdom Awards. She was a runner-up for the Cinnamon Press Novel Competition. She received her MA in Creative Writing from Trinity College, Carmarthen, and her PhD from Aberystwyth University's Creative Writing program.

Paula R. C. Readman lives in a quiet village in Essex, with her hard-working husband, Russell, who allows her to follow her dream. In 2010, she had her first success with writing fiction when English Heritage published her story in *Whitby Abbey – Pure Inspiration*, since then she has won two writing competitions, including having her story, 'Roofscapes' selected as the overall winner by best-selling crime writer Mark Billingham and has had several other short stories published too. Find her at paulareadman1.wordpress.com

Laura Wilkinson is a writer, reader, wife and mother to ginger boys. As well as writing fiction, she works as an editor for literary consultancy, Cornerstones. Laura has published short stories in magazines, digital media and anthologies, and two novels. *Public Battles, Private Wars* (Accent Press) is the story of a young miner's wife in 1984; of friends and rivals; loving and fighting, and being the best you can be. For more information, visit: laura-wilkinson. co.uk or follow her on Facebook, Laura Wilkinson Author, or Twitter @ScorpioScribble.

Rhys Owain Williams was born and raised in Morriston, Swansea. Having completed an English with Creative Writing degree at Swansea University, he continued to study there for an MA in Creative Writing (2009–10). Rhys has published in various magazines, and was one of forty poets to be featured in Wales' first ever national anthology of haiku poetry, *Another Country* (Gomer), in 2011. He is a regular reader at spoken-word events across south Wales.

Editors

Rebecca Parfitt is a writer who has been published in numerous anthologies and magazines. She has worked in publishing for eight years. She is Editor of *The Ghastling*, a magazine devoted to ghost stories and the macabre which she set up in 2013 inspired by her love of the dark and peculiar. In her spare time she can be found climbing the ropes at the circus.

Claire Houguez cheerily (wo)mans Parthian's Swansea University office. She joined Parthian as a jack of all trades in 2010, and looks after ebooks and marketing, with some design and editing. She is a graduate of Swansea Metropolitan University and Swansea University, where she received a Distinction in her Creative Writing MA. She is working towards a PhD with a fiction collection capturing the neo-burlesque revival – the research for which has become a bit clothes-off.

PARTHIAN

Three women, three generations: one dark secret...

A novel about the tangled, often dysfunctional, bonds of family; about soothing yourself with fairytales instead of challenging yourself to live with reality.

"Mysterious, esoteric and compassionate..." *Buzz Magazine*

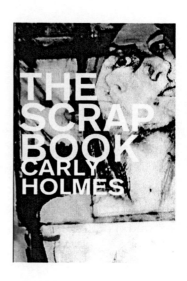

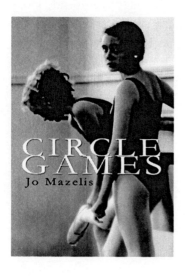

Competing claims – and flawed, elusive love – are the territory of these nineteen rich stories. *Circle Games* probes our darker fantasies of power, control and revenge, in a world not far removed from Grimm's menacing forests, where games are seldom innocent.

"dark, disconcerting and full of surprises" *Sullen Art*

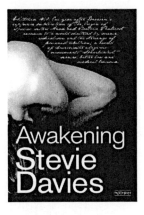